Other Books By Sean McDonough

Available Now!

Beverly Kills

The Terror At Turtleshell Mountain

1

Mike didn't want to open his eyes. Not with his head throbbing like it was. Not while his limbs felt like they were weighed down with iron chains. Every inch of his body was either sore, bruised, or burning. The surface under his back felt hard. Gritty. Jesus Christ, had he slept in the fucking *parking lot*?

He gritted his teeth. *All right, man up. Open your eyes and let's check out the damage.*

His punishment was swift and severe. The mere thought of moving stirred up the fury of the hangover beasts nesting in the ruins of his head. Mike tried to close his eyes even tighter, as if in apology, but the roaring thing the inside of his skull showed him no mercy.

Please, he moaned. *I take it back. I'll stay here. I'll sleep in the parking lot.* Anything. Whatever it took to quiet the snarling agony in his head, that's what he would do. He'd live in the parking lot. Give up his trailer. Sell his-

His keys! His eyes bulged beneath his closed eyelids. Where the hell were his keys!? He couldn't feel them in his pants pockets. That left only his jacket packet. If he was lucky.

Please. Please, let me be lucky.

Eyes closed, he summoned all of his will and prepared to move his arm. Just a little. Just far enough to pat his pocket. *Please God,* he thought, *I've suffered enough. Just let me still have my truck keys.*

Mike wiggled his fingers. Winced. Fuck, it was only going to get worse; but there was nothing else for it. He braced himself. *1... 2...*

His arm rattled. Something heavy shuffled along with his wrist. He registered something cold clamped around his wrist... a bracelet? Another blackout mystery waiting to be solved. His text messages were going to be hilarious.

IF I still have my phone, that is.

Only one way to find out. Mike summoned all of his will and finally did it. He opened his eyes. He looked around and discovered that there were worse things than pain in this world. Worse things than missing truck keys.

There were memories.

We went to the Hangar Bar after work. Me, Zee, Joe Scro, and that blonde chick with the ink that Zee's always trying to hook up with. Car bombs? Hell yes. I'd been working double shifts all week and the only thing I wanted to do was throw twenty dollars into the jukebox, hang out with my friends, and get completely fucked up.

And then THEY came.

THEM.

Mike remembered everything now. And if he there was anything he'd forgotten, the scene before his eyes filled in way too many blanks. The Hangar Bar, his second home since his first fake ID, was in flames. Every window was shattered. The jukebox lay upside down on the smoldering porch.

The bodies were everywhere. The bartenders were impaled on the decorative propeller blades mounted over the door. Some other poor bastard lay draped over a smashed windowsill. His blood ran down the wall and pooled on the boards beneath his carcass.

Zee had finally gotten that blonde after all. Her severed head rested between his legs.

Where Zee's head was, Mike had no idea.

Mike leapt up. His keys didn't matter. *Run. Run before THEY realize someone's still alive.* That was his intention, except he could not leap. He couldn't even stand. His limbs would not allow it. He could do nothing but thrash and flop on the asphalt like a fish choking on air.

He thought he could get away? They already had him. They'd gotten him before he'd even woken up.

They had him lying spread-eagle in the parking lot, held in place by lengths of chains shackled to his wrists and ankles.

At the far end of each chain was an automobile. A Dodge Ram shackled to his right arm. A Porsche Boxster chained to his left arm. A Cadillac

Escalade strapped to one leg. And a real beaut, a 1973 Mustang Mach 1, cuffed to his other leg. Each vehicle was pure, matte black. Each one was aimed at a different point of the compass.

Each one stood idling, just waiting for a foot to step on the gas.

Mike understood then. He screamed and writhed as much as his chains would allow.

But not enough to get free. Never enough to get away.

"NOO!" he begged. "DON'T! PLEASE! PLEASE DON'T DO IT!"

The only response was music drifting from the open window of the Ram truck. George Thorogood and the Destroyers. *Who Do You Love?*

The engines revved. The lurking power of thirty-two combined cylinders snorted and rumbled in the silence of the night, begging to be let loose. The rumbling roadhouse guitar blasted right alongside it.

Mike screamed almost as loudly.

Cued by some silent signal, the cars and trucks bellowed together. Tires squealed.

They peeled out to the four points. North, South, East, and West. The meager slack in the chains disappeared in less than two seconds. Mike was lifted. His limbs pulled taut and then flew apart. The roaring vehicles ripped Mike's limbs from their sockets and left him a bleeding square of meat, mewling out his last breath on the dirty asphalt.

Which isn't to say that it wasn't exceedingly painful for the few moments that Mike lingered alongside the living.

The vehicles drove on, Mike's limbs flapping off their bumpers like wedding streamers. As they faded into the night, George Thorogood wailed out from the darkness, asking the same question just one more time:

"Who do you love?"

2

From *Rolling Stone* magazine, November 5th, 2005. Interview of Jackie Galindo by Djavan Dean:

"Rock and Roll?" he says. "Rock and Roll is the Death Trip."

He laughs at my surprise. He already has his skull-face makeup on (neon green and black this time. A Day of the Dead skeleton from raver hell), and when he smiles the effect is like a mouth smiling within another mouth. *Aliens* by way of Guillermo Del Toro. I tell him as much and that double smile just gets wider. This is obviously the kind of compliment Jackie Galindo loves to hear.

But I don't want to get too far away from the point he just made. I ask him what he means when he calls Rock and Roll, his lifeblood and mine, "the Death Trip."

"Exactly what I said," he responds. "It's music for the suicidal, the terminal, and the homicidal."

"AC/DC, *Long Way to the Top if You Wanna Rock and Roll*," I challenge. "Motley Crue, *Kickstart My Heart.* Iggy Pop, *Lust for Life.*"

"Death," Jackie says. "Death, death, and, oh yeah, death."

I was in the crowd when Ozzy bit the head off of that live bat. I know how to react to that. I know how to respond to musicians who want to do an interview in the nude or give their responses in between lines of blow. I know what those guys want and I know better than to give it to them.

I don't know how to respond to this. Part of me wonders if I'm talking to Pat Robertson masquerading in Jackie Galindo's green and black skeleton makeup. But then he laughs at my discomfort and there's too much arrogant, contemptuous glee in that cackle for this to be anything but the genuine article.

"Iggy, Bon, Vince. Did any of those guys make responsible life choices? No! It's a bald-ass miracle two out of the three are still alive. And that's what they sang about. Rock and Roll is about not giving a fuck if you live or die. It's about going as hard as you can as fast as you can... and if you lose your head for it, then so what?"

He leans forward and there's a mad gleam in his eye. I'd call it Devil May Care but Jackie Galindo is the Devil and it's obvious that he does not care. "You can make Rock and Roll about having a good time," he says. "I've made a lot of money that way. You can make Rock and Roll about being in love or getting dumped or any other emotion on the wheel of life. But that's all shared real estate. You want to feel good? You can go to country music, rap music, pop, or your local pharmacist. It's common ground.

"But when you're riding the bomb all the way to ground zero, when you're going to a gun fight and all you're bringing is your *teeth*, when you know the end is coming but you're determined to go out with a smile and as many motherfuckers as you can take for company... that's when nothing else will do the trick. That's when the only thing you've got on this earth is Rock and Roll."

I've done my best to reproduce the gravity of his words, but I don't know if I can. There's an impact that can only come with sharing a room with Jackie Galindo. Looking at him, it's easy to believe that the painted skull is all there is and there's no human face behind it.

"Well, Jack."

"Jackie," he interrupts me. " Always Jackie. Jack is what it says on my taxes. "

"Well, Jackie," I correct myself. "...It sounds like this "Death Trip" is a philosophy you've put a lot of thought into."

Jackie leans back in his seat. The better to grab the open bottle of Jim Beam on the corner table.

"Nah, not really," he says.

3

Elle trusted her phone's GPS to guide her through the unfamiliar curves of the Hollywood Hills.

She trusted in a God that she technically didn't believe in to keep the wheezy Firebird from breaking down before she got where she was going.

And why wouldn't she? God may not exist, but she still had more faith in him than she did in Joe Abner's "Six Month Lemon Fresh Guarantee."

As if to prove her point, the car's AC system sputtered, coughed, and then ran lukewarm.

Great.

Elle rolled down the window using an honest to God crankshaft. She watched the four million dollar homes roll by and wondered, not for the first time, which one of these millionaires had called all the way out to Santa Clarita for this rolling crap bucket.

Stupid question. She had the name on the address slip Abner had given to her. The same name that had been running laps around her shaved head ever since she had left the valley.

It's not really him.

It can't be.

It wasn't even the right name. "Jack" Galindo. Jack, not Jackie.

And it's always Jackie. Always. He said it himself.

Besides, it wasn't like Jack Galindo was that exotic of a name. There were probably hundreds of them.

The GPS brought her to 20 Saturn Road and announced she had reached her destination: a luxurious, old-style stucco manor. There was a "For Sale" sign posted in the grassless, sustainable front yard. Elle didn't even want to guess how much it went for.

She shifted into park. Looked at the house. *Jack Galindo,* she repeated to herself. *Just Jack.* She stepped out of the car. *Probably some dentist sick of people always asking him if he's that weirdo in the skull makeup.*

So she told herself. And then she took off her denim jacket and threw it on the passenger seat She wore a t-shirt underneath. No sleeves, the better to show off the thorn branch tattoos running up and down her arms. And no midriff, the better to display the tipped-over whiskey bottle tattooed below her breasts.

"Keep your jacket on. Try to look respectable for God's sake," Abner had said. Well, fuck him. Like he was ever going to know. She opened her purse and fastened her nose studs and lip ring back into place.

Okay, it probably wasn't *HIM.* But… if it was, well, then Elle wasn't about to knock on Jackie Galindo's door dressed like some chump norm who cleaned out used cars for a living. No, she wanted to come before him as the bassist from MurderCycle Diaries, and as a pilgrim on the path of the Rock and Roll Death Trip.

You're just setting yourself up to get let down.

Maybe. But no matter what she told herself, she grew more and more anxious with every step that brought her closer to the front door.

"Tracy, wait!"

She heard the voice clearly through the door. It was shrill and toothless. A beggar's voice.

Elle slowed her roll. *That's not Jackie Galindo.* No way. That was some puss-ass studio exec pleading after his little fuck-puppet while she left him for a fatter wallet.

"You weren't even supposed to be here, Jack! I could come and get my things and not have to see you. You promised me!"

Ah, and there was the fuck-puppet. Just as Elle expected. Along with the drama, she could hear the echo of stamping feet over stone tile.

"I'm sorry!" the wimp pleaded.

"Fuck your sorry!" The fuck-puppet screeched back. "I didn't ask for it. I didn't ask for anything except not to hear another one of your fucking lies!"

"I know that I fucked up. But I love you-"

"You don't go behind somebody's back if you love them!"

"Just stop for a second!" He cried, so loud Elle might as well have been in the room with him. So agonized, you'd think he was getting eviscerated instead of dumped.

Elle hesitated before knocking. Maybe she should do a lap and hope the Real Ex-housewife was gone before she came back.

And then the door flew open and made the decision for her. A blonde came storming out with a foo-foo dog tucked under one arm and a carrier full of dog crap under the other.

"It's over!" the blonde screamed. She didn't slow down. Didn't look back over her shoulder. "Stop calling me! Stop texting me! Stop trying to see me!"

She didn't even acknowledge Elle. Just kept right on moving. Elle didn't even have time to get a good look at her as she swept by.

But you saw enough, didn't you? Enough to think you've seen her before.

But the thought fled as soon as it appeared. All thoughts fled as *he* came running down the stairs. He wasn't wearing his skeleton facepaint, but it didn't matter. Elle recognized the rattlesnake tattoo wrapped around his neck. She even had his piercings memorized- a curved scimitar dangling from one earlobe, and the horned devil head stud in the cartilage of his other ear.

JACKIE GALINDO!

"Tracy, please wait!" Jack screamed.

Tracy did not wait. She put the dog and the carrier into the back of a Tesla, and her only response was a slamming door and the high whirring of the engine as she sped off.

Elle didn't move. Didn't speak.

Oh my God. Oh shit. Oh shit. It was him! Really him! He was right in front of her!

…Wasn't he?

Elle's phone background was a picture of Jackie Galindo at Ozzfest '06- Jackie Galindo in red and black skullface, mouth forever frozen in an eternal scream of fury. She had the cover art from *Sulfuric Messiah* tattooed between her shoulder blades- Jackie Galindo crawling out of a rancid yellow cloud with a machete clenched between his teeth.

The guy in front of her had the right tattoos. He had the right piercings. He was thin but wiry, like he was built out of pipe cleaners and copper. Mid-thirties? Check. Mexican? Check. Same deep-set eyes and shaved head? Check and check.

So then how was it that she didn't recognize him at all?

Elle snapped out of her musings, realizing that she'd been blatantly staring at him for almost a minute; and then realizing that she'd been staring at him for almost an entire sixty seconds and he hadn't even noticed her.

Elle coughed to get his attention. *He'll turn and I'll be able to look him in the eyes. That will settle it. I'll know then.*

The man didn't react. He stayed at the curb, staring at the curve in the road the blonde woman had disappeared around. He stood perfectly still. Like a wax figure.

"Uh… excuse me?" she said.

The wax figure moved. He shuddered up from whatever private world he'd been in and noticed Elle for the first time.

He still didn't say anything. He surveyed her with dull eyes. His mouth hung slightly ajar. Elle wanted desperately to reach out and close it, but she couldn't bring herself to touch him.

Because what if I touch him and it's not skin that I feel?

"Are you Mr. Galindo? I'm from Abner Automobiles. I'm here with your 2002 Firebird?"

His disinterested gaze sharpened briefly then.

"Right," he said. He finally saw the silver Pontiac. The same silver Pontiac that had been right in front of him the whole time he'd been… wherever it was he'd gone. He walked towards the car and Elle followed, unsure of if she was supposed to or not. This whole deal was weird, even before the Jackie Galindo/Not Jackie Galindo business. Joe Abner never did deals over the phone. He never complained about Elle's "presentability," and he never did business with big shakers in LA.

She hung back and watched awkwardly as he popped the hood and inspected the engine. He was silent again, but his eyes were closer now. More present. Elle got the impression there was nothing he wasn't noticing now.

He slammed the hood closed. "It'll work," he said.

"Great!" Elle said. Inwardly, she winced. Her enthusiasm sounded fake, even to herself.

He held out a set of keys to her, and now it was Elle's turn to stare. What? Why was he-

"He's going to give you a trade-in," Abner said. *"The title's already signed. Just take the keys and bring it back. And God help you if there's so much as a scratch, Elle. I mean it."*

"Right!" Elle blundered. She took the keys from him. "And it's…"

He pointed past her shoulder. Towards the driveway.

Fucking duh, Elle thought. She spun, following the line of his finger.

…Jesus Christ.

He had a red and black SRT Challenger Hellcat. Freshly polished and gleaming in the sun like red lightening.

"You want to trade…*that,*" Elle said. "For this?" She swiveled back towards the Firebird on its retread tires.

"That was the deal," he said.

"And how many other cars!?" Elle shrieked.

He did not smile back at her. "Are the keys inside the Firebird?" he asked.

"Yeah," she said. "In the ignition." She regretted saying anything now. The longer this conversation went on, the more she felt like one of them didn't really exist. That this whole conversation was between one person and a figment of their imagination.

Worse, Elle was beginning to fear that she was the figment.

"Well," she said. "If there's nothing else…"

He sighed. He looked down the road again and was met with the same nobody looking back at him.

"No," he said. "Nothing else."

To her own surprise, Elle felt no desire to twist back for a final look at him as she walked away. She didn't even take the time to appreciate the Challenger's sleek interior or the eager rumble of its engine when she cranked the ignition. She wanted to be gone. If this empty husk was what lurked

Behind the Music, Elle hoped that she never made it big.

She shifted into reverse and rode the brake down the long driveway. She realized her jacket and charger were still in the Firebird. It didn't matter. She kept going.

Her phone buzzed. Grateful for the distraction, she fished it out.

The car horn blared in her ear. Elle screamed. She dropped the phone and slammed on the brakes on instinct, just in time to stop from plastering a fucking Maserati as it pulled up to the curb.

Shit! Shit! Shit!

The driver got out. Certainly to rip Elle a new one.

…Except he didn't. His focus seemed to be on the Firebird and the man standing next to it. Once again, it was as if she weren't there at all.

This time, Elle didn't mind it. She finished backing out of the driveway and got the hell back onto the road. It wasn't until she was sitting at a red light at the base of that she dared to pick her phone up off the floor.

She had a text from her friend, and drummer, Vickie:

Was it him!?!?

With everything that happened, Elle had to think for a second to remember that she'd texted Vickie before heading to (maybe) Jackie Galindo's house. Of course, Vickie had gotten tired of waiting and needed to know if it had really been THAT Jackie Galindo

Without thinking, Elle typed out her response and hit "Send."

No... Not him.

4

"You're lucky that kid missed me," Luke called out. "I mean, yeah, you weren't the one driving, but your car? Pulling out of your property? You'd need to get me to call your lawyer and inform him that he was going to be hearing from *my* lawyer." He grinned. Jack did not grin back, but he was not caught off guard by this new arrival. This man, with his neatly trimmed blonde hair, Savile Row suit, and his sunglasses worth more than the Pontiac behind him, was a well-known quantity.

He was also the last person in the world Jack wanted to see.

"What are you doing here, Luke?"

"Checking up on my favorite client."

Jack shrugged. Held his arms out. "I'm here. Alive. Well. I told you to wait for me to call you."

"And I told you to give Tracy some space," Luke said. "Or are you going to try and tell me that wasn't her car I saw whizzing by on the way up here?"

Jack didn't answer.

"I did tell you," Luke said.

"And I told you to leave me alone," Jack snapped back.

"How am I supposed to do that when I know this is what you get up to when I leave you unsupervised?" He gestured wildly at the Firebird. "That thing is tetanus on wheels, Jack. In five miles it's going to be tetanus broken down on the side of the road."

"I know how an engine's supposed to look," Jack said. "When I was sixteen my dad got me a socket wrench set and a Cavalier up on blocks. Not a BMW and a AAA card."

Luke raised a hand to shield his heart. "Hurtful, Jack. Truthful, but hurtful."

"If it's true then that's one more reason for you to turn back around. I'm not going on your kind of vacation."

"Yeah, you told me. All that poor, wayfaring stranger crap. But, here's the swerve… I actually love it. Really, I do. I think you're sitting on a concept

album and you don't even realize it. So-
"

"Luke."

"SO, since you put your assistant on paid vacation, you're going to need someone to tag along and take notes. That way, six months from now when all of this is behind you and you're back in the studio, you won't have to say, 'Gee, what barren piece of wasteland was I drifting past when-"

"LUKE."

Luke sighed. All of his swagger and slickness went out with it.

"You really want to make me say it? Fine. When you signed with me, you were a nobody and I was only slightly less of a nobody. Fast forward two years, and you got huge and plenty of big shot agents wanted to represent you. Now, we both said a lot of bullshit about how I was the one who knew your career best… but we both know the real reason you stayed with me is because we're friends."

Luke took off his sunglasses. "That kind of means you're stuck with me, Jack."

"I don't need a chaperone. I'm fine, Luke."

"Jack, if you were sixteen your Instagram would be full of black and white pictures tagged with bullshit 'I'm so sad, I want to kill myself' lyrics. I'm not asking you if you're okay. I'm telling you that you're not."

Jack opened his mouth-

"And of course you're going to disagree," Luke cut in, "And I'm not going to waste time convincing you otherwise. Instead, as a counterproposal, how about we both pretend that I'm the fucked up one?"

Luke grinned and shuffled. "What do you say? I'm all broken up because… I don't know, because that intern in my office with the Katy Perry tits took a job at CAA. It's got me all torn up and now I'm begging you Jack, *begging you*. Please, please, please let me come with you on your desert quest for understanding and wisdom and probably diarrhea from all that bad food."

Then, to show how sincere he was, Luke got down on his knees. Right there in his Savile suit. He raised his hands in supplication, praying for favor from Jackie Galindo, *El Diablo de Dia Los Muertos.*

"Go home, Luke," Jack said.

Jack went back to the house. He slammed the door without so much as a single backwards glance.

It was cold inside of the house. Partly because of the central AC. Mostly from the bitter cold Tracy had left in her wake.

"Give Tracy some space," Luke had said. And Jack believed that he had. He hadn't spoken to her in a week. A week where it felt like he had fire ants living under his skin. He was there because he thought that if she would give him two minutes, two minutes just to fucking *explain* what had happened.

She hadn't. She'd done nothing but assure him that what he'd done was unforgivable. And that she would never, EVER love him again.

He shook his head. He hadn't come inside for a recap. His beat up old duffle bag was right where he'd left it, by the door. Just in case things with Tracy didn't…

The bag had no designer label on the front. There was nothing "artfully" distressed about it. It was an old bag from a cheap store; made older and cheaper by many years of hard use. It waited for him at the base of the glass display case housing a black 1968 Les Paul.

Normally, Jack thought that sticking a guitar in a case was about as appropriate as sticking a tiger in a cage. He made an exception because this guitar was special. The black Les had been a gift from his first label. He'd taken it on his first national tour, played it across 40 cities in 30 states, and walked away thinking it was the most sublime instrument he'd ever held.

With the money from that first record deal, the first thing he'd done was buy his parents a new house. Then he bought himself a house. And then he'd bought a glass display case for the Les Paul and promised himself that one day, fifty years in the future when he was ready to retire, he would bring the Les back out for one final victory lap.

So the guitar wasn't a tiger in a cage. It was a dragon in hibernation.

Waiting for the perfect moment to rise up and bring about the end of the world.

Jack reached for the duffle bag and his knuckles slipped readily into the grooves worn into the strap. It should have felt good, like turning back the clock, but he barely even noticed. He was too enraptured by the sight of his own reflection staring back at him from the glass case.

Truthfully, it was barely even his reflection. The glass was not a mirror. All he saw was little more than the translucent lines of his face and eyes overlaid against the body of the ebony Les Paul guitar. Besides, he'd seen his reflection somewhere recently, hadn't he? He must have. He knew what he looked like.

Jack lashed out with both hands. He pushed at that ghostly reflection, pushed it away with all the force he could summon, but it was the case that fell over backwards. It hit the stone floor and shattered, smashing his reflection and throwing broken glass everywhere.

It never occurred to Jack to clean up the shards, nobody would be in the house until he came back, but he did consider sparing the moment it would take to pick up the guitar. There was something obscene about seeing the Les Paul lying string-side down in the glass like that.

You're not going to leave it like that, are you? The first time you picked that baby up it felt like you were getting knighted.

At the very least, he should check it for scratches.

...Fuck it. Jack grabbed the duffle bag and slammed the door behind him. He left the guitar lying there amongst the ruins.

5

Luke was back on his feet, but he was still waiting by the curb when Jack came out of the house. Of course he was. Tenacity was part of what Jack paid him for.

Had he heard the crash of the display case falling over? Probably. Attention to detail was another part of his job description.

Looking the other way also comes with the territory.

"Go home, Luke," Jack said as he brushed by him.

Jack threw his bag into the trunk and went back around to the driver's side. His gaze stayed firmly fixed ahead. He did not spare a look towards Luke. Still waiting in his front yard. Still not looking the other way.

Jack put one foot into the Firebird but stopped short of bringing in the other one. He stood there, one foot in, one foot out, and heaved a heavy sigh.

"Last call," he said.

It took Luke a second, but then he grinned broadly. It was not the grin he used on talent and executives, it was the grin he used when his elementary school best friend came over with *Super Mario 2.*

"Just let me get my suitcase!"

While Luke went for his baggage, Jack settled into the Firebird. Cloth seats instead of leather. No "connectivity" except for an auxiliary audio jack. Absolutely no new car scent at all, just the lingering dusty musk that came with months, maybe years, of sitting out beneath the San Fernando Valley sun.

Jack loved it.

He turned on the radio, just to see what the pre-sets were. *Kroq and JackFM,* he figured. *Maybe GoCountry.* Whatever it was, checking the radio pre-sets was like skimming the surface of somebody's soul.

What he got was the KIIS FM Morning Show with Brett and Britt.

"-From our 'Who Didn't See That One Coming?' file, reps from both have confirmed that this year's Super Bowl half-time performer Tracee Trance and shock rocker Jackie Galindo have called it quits."

"Oh, no!" Britt chimed in.

Brett's response was to play an Emma Stone soundbite:

"I'm sorry, were you dropped on your head as an infant?"

"You're kidding, right?" Brett asked.

"They just seemed like they were really in love," she protested.

"Come on, Tracee Trance is on the wall of every thirteen-year-old girl in the country. Jackie Galindo dresses up like Donald Trump's worst nightmare and once set himself on fire, *on stage,* because he didn't think the crowd was loud enough. That kind of thing is fun for a while, but what kind of life do you think you're going to-"

Jack punched the power button, wishing that it was actually Brett Rice's teeth beneath his knuckles. *Not so noble when you were trying to coax a blowjob from 20 year old wannabes at the Universal Records Christmas party, were you, Brett?* Jack fumed. He was still seething when Luke came strolling back, rolling an Armani suitcase behind him. He placed the bag into the trunk and slid into the passenger seat.

"Tell me something," Luke said. "The dead lizard dried up in the back, did you pay extra for that?" He chuckled as he reached for the radio dial.

"Leave it off," Jack snapped.

"Couldn't agree more," Luke said, cheerfully oblivious. "FM radio? We'll hear *Times Like These* until our ears bleed." He dangled an auxiliary cord from one finger. "But can I run a playlist? Or are we supposed to sit in silence and listen for whispered secrets from the cacti?"

"Plug it in, smartass," Jack said. He shifted the car into gear while Luke fiddled with cables and ports.

"So where are we going?" Luke asked.

"North," Jack said with a shrug. "We'll probably cut east once we hit the One Thirty-Four."

"And then what?"

Jack smiled. "Luke, we'll take it as it comes."

Luke put his sunglasses back on. "Well, I was up until three AM partying

with Emily Rat… Rata…Rattamana…
fuck it, you know who I mean. Point is
I'll leave you to it, Captain. Wake me
up when we get to the Middle of
Nowhere." He folded his arms across
his chest and put his feet up on the
dashboard. He was asleep a few
moments later.

Listening to Luke's deviated
septum whistle, Jack reflected that it
might be nice to have Luke with him
after all. He really was a friend, not just
an agent. And beneath the manicures
and tailored suits, there actually was a
little bark on his tree. It was possible he
might even enjoy himself.

But making his way through the
traffic on the One Thirty-Four freeway,
Jack was grateful that Luke was asleep
and he could feel like he had some
solitude. Keeping one eye on the road,
he woke up Luke's iPhone and cycled
through the playlists. He knew what he
was looking for, and he found it tucked
in between *Fucking (FWBs Only)* and
Molly Mix.

Jack's Crap.
Jack hit play.

The music that came from the blown-out speakers was not the kind of music Jackie Galindo performed. No shredding guitars cranked to 11; no vocals like the furious screeching of an automobile collision.

What came out instead was the kind of music Jack Galindo liked to listen to. Jason Molina, Mary Gauthier, and the Drive-by Truckers. Lonesome guitar chords and vocalists that didn't so much sing as they did mourn. It was the music of bars furnished with wood marred by 30 years of cigarette burns and air that smelled of spilled drinks and forgotten hopes. Luke made his jokes, but it was the music of coyotes with a hundred empty miles ahead of them and a thousand empty miles behind them.

It was the music of peaceful emptiness, and that was what Jack craved as the traffic thinned and he saw the ramp for Route 2 heading north.

But the Two was just the beginning. The Two would take them through the Angeles Forest and lead them to the One Thirty-Eight.

And the One Thirty-Eight was the desert.

"You can ski in the morning and surf in the afternoon." That's one of the most oft-repeated perks of living in southern California. It's possible to have breakfast on the snow-capped mountains of Big Bear and then do lunch by the Pacific Ocean in Santa Monica.

What everyone overlooks is that, just as close as the snow or the surf, there is the desert.

And that's the way the desert likes it. The desert is not made for the masses. The desert likes to be forgotten because its silence and desolation, its essence, is weakened by the presence of too many people.

But alone? Alone, the desert can take you in and wipe everything else from your mind. Go far enough into the heat and the dust and everything beyond its borders ceases to exist, and all that's left is peace.

Entering the Angeles National Forest, he spied a *No Littering* sign posted just before the first canyon. Jack had been raised better than that, but in a sense littering was exactly what this trip was about. Jack had too much garbage in his mind and in his heart, and he aimed to cast as much of it to the side of the road as he could.

The Firebird rolled on, an insignificant speck of silver on a slope of rock that had stood for thousands of years with the sun bright overhead. There were trees in the canyon, and scrub brush clinging gamely along the side of the road, but the rocks and heat took up more and more real estate with every passing mile. Soon, the desert would be all that there was.

Jack sensed it coming and felt lighter already.

6

That night, they stopped for dinner at a diner somewhere north of Bakersfield. The sign outside hadn't been replaced since the 1970s. In LA, it would have been called vintage. Out here, it was just cheaper not to buy a new sign.

Inside, there was no wait to sit and no wait to order. Jack had a steak sandwich. Luke had a burger. Then a pot pie. Then another burger. Jack watched his friend dig into his third helping and tried to hide his amusement. "Not bad, huh?" he asked.

"The obesity epidemic in this country makes a lot more sense now." Luke washed down the last of his chili cheese fries with a gulp of Sprite. "You ever been here before?"

Jack shook his head. "Not this place, but a dozen like it. Back in my not-college days I'd hit the road like this all the time." He waved a hand out the diner window, out to the rocks and darkness beyond the glass. "Pick a direction and go," he said. "No maps, no destinations, free as the bird you cannot change. Half of what I know about music, I learned from guys playing in nowhere towns just like this," He sighed, lost in memories of bars that didn't bother to card and forty-year-old truck drivers and ranchers who didn't care about anything but just getting a chance to fucking *play*.

Jack picked up his Coke but didn't drink. He stared into it like he was waiting for something to rise up from the dark well of the cup. "Some time after you got me on the dotted line, I stopped getting out here." He shook his head ruefully. "Too busy with press tours and launch parties to find time for the things that made me in the first place."

"Yeah, yeah," Luke drawled. "Let me wipe away my tears with a hundred dollar bill." He took another bite from his burger. "But while we're on memory lane, let me ask-" he gestured to the food spread out in front of them, "Was this always a happy meal?"

"What do you mean?" Jack asked.

"I mean, did your urge to become a rambling man kick up a notch every time some blue-eyed rancher's daughter gave your heart a kick in the nuts?"

Jack shrugged. His eyes stayed focused on his cup. "Maybe once or twice. Driving helps me sort things out."

"Sorted yet?"

Jack looked up from the Coke then. "Don't rush me, Luke," he warned.

Luke held his hands up. "Not rushing, just trying to get an idea of our estimated flight time. We've been on the road seven hours and we're up four hundred and twelve miles on the odometer. Just tell me who the record holder is."

Jack considered. "Becky Lambert, I guess. Summer after high school. Must have been fourteen hundred miles over four days."

Luke whistled. "Think we're going to beat that?"

Jack fell silent, tracing imaginary maps across America and across his heart. Finally, he nodded. "Probably."

Then it was Luke's turn to consider. His mind, not an artist's, worked differently than Jack's. Luke's head was a calculator- crunching numbers and running algorithms. It took in all the data, calculated it, double-checked its findings, and came to a conclusion.

"Hm," he said.

"Hm, what?"

"Hm, what the hell could you have cared about so much that you'd be willing to risk making that girl leave you?"

"You want to walk home?" Jack threatened.

"I'm just trying to figure out what happened. You won't tell me so I'm stuck trying to piece it together on my own."

"She's done with me. That's all you need to know."

Luke leaned across the table. "No, not all I need to know. That girl was nuts for you, Jack. If she ended it, that means there's a hell of a thing wrong with you that I don't know about. It's my job to take care of you. I can't do that if you're hiding things from me."

"It's your job to do whatever I tell you to do," Jack said. "And I'm telling you if you bring this up again, then you can find yourself a ride back to LA."

He wasn't bluffing. In the silence that followed, Luke saw his real client for the first time since this whole mess with Tracy started. Jackie Galindo-head hung low, dark eyes cast into shadow, hands knotted into tight fists on the tabletop.

Jack was not really a fan of the type of music he created. There was no Motorhead, Black Sabbath, or Misfits on any of his personal playlists. He could pitch as many acoustic, stripped down albums as he wanted, but the truth was that Jackie Galindo's sound always was and always would be nothing but electric thunder set against a voice like a blender on high.

And this face right here was the reason why. It didn't matter what you liked to hear in your own ears, great music came from the gut and Jackie Galindo's guts were filled with nothing but fire and molten iron. You always saw it when he played, but Luke saw it now too, bubbling up behind Jackie's clenched teeth, desperate to burst loose.

And when that fire and liquid metal started flowing, you either got out of its way or you got burned alive.

So Luke got out of the way.

"Okay," he said. "Whatever you say, boss." He waved for the check. Their waitress brought it over, a fifty-year-old woman who looked like she'd never worked anywhere else in her life and didn't particularly seem to mind. She brought the bill over on a dented, faded plastic tray that had probably been there longer than she had. Luke slapped down a hundred dollar bill without even looking at the total. He stood up and slipped on his blazer.

"Come on, Jackie. Let's chase some telephone poles."

Jack didn't laugh. They left the diner in silence; the only sound between them was the phantom static of whatever memories Luke had stirred up.

Luke looked at Jackie's back, wiry shoulders hunched in tight, and shook his head. Not because he was worried about getting fired, but because his job was to make things better for Jack, not worse.

So? Make things better. Earn your commission.

"Hey!" he blurted out. "Let me drive a little, yeah? I want to double back to that last fork before we hit the diner. I got a feeling there's something worth checking out down the left hand pass or whatever. Maybe even a strip joint if we're lucky. One where everybody still has their teeth if we're really lucky."

Jack's scowl bent but didn't break. "Did you look that up on your phone?"

"Not the part about the strip club," Luke said. "But if we do find one, I you're your Russian roulette, 'take it as it comes' attitude won't object to a little research about the whole 'teeth' thing."

Jack's grin cracked through for real this time. He threw Luke the keys. "You're starting to get the hang of this."

"Not bad for a spoiled city boy."

They got into the car and turned pulled out of the lot.

A moment after they faded into the distance, four more cars pulled into the lot. A Porsche, an old Mustang, an Escalade, and a Ram Truck. All four vehicles were as dark and sheenless as the fur of a black wolf, and their engines grumbled just as ferociously.

-   -   -

Jack and Luke's waitress' name was Anna. Contrary to what Luke thought, she actually had lived elsewhere. Back in 1984, she and two friends had thrown everything they owned into a Toyota Camry and went out to Los Angeles in search of fame and fortune. In eight months, they got exactly one gig- a hundred bucks each to be bikini girls in a Motley Crue video. Her friends had a blast and vowed to never leave. Anna got puked on by Vince Neil, went back home to work in her father's diner, and never once questioned if she made the right decision.

She was manager and part owner these days. She could spend every shift sitting in the small office next to the walk-in cooler if she so desired, but she still liked to occasionally come out and spend an hour manning the tables.

First were those two boys, LA boys if she'd ever seen two. And now here was a family of three. Young parents and a four-year-old boy. Anna smiled to herself. A first born obviously, he had that swagger about him and he had his mother and father scurrying about, clearly seeking his favor.

"Look, buddy! Check out all of those old pictures on the wall!"

"See the burger that girl has, Eric? Doesn't that look good?!"

Not that Anna was judging the child. Little prince he may have been, the boy was smiling and holding his parents hands, not kicking or throwing food everywhere, and that went a long way in Anna McCarthy's book. She went up to their table with her order pad in hand. "You folks coming or going?" she asked.

"Coming back," the father said. "Just made it out to the Grand Canyon."

Anna's eyes got wide, stretching out a little of that marginal acting talent she never put to use in LA. "Just? You don't *just* go out to the Grand Canyon! You say 'Oh my God! We came *all the way back* from the GRAND CANYON!" She fixed her attention on the little boy. "You must be starving! I hope you at least had some snacks in the car."

The boy, not such a little tyrant after all, grinned bashfully and couldn't look her in the eye. "Cookies," he mumbled.

"Cookies?!" she exclaimed. "You can't expect a growing boy to make it all the way back from the Grand Canyon on just *cookies!* You look to me like you could use a milkshake. Does that sound about right?"

The boy looked to his mother first. "Go ahead, Eric," she said.

Permission granted, he beamed at Anna and held up two fingers. "Two, please!" he shouted.

"Coming right up," Anna said. "What else can I get you folks?" She took their orders and then went back into the kitchen, still smiling and shaking her head.

The smell hit her even before she made it through the swinging door, tantalizing hints riding the breeze out from under the door. Rodrigo had said he was going to experiment with some new barbecue sauces but God, something smelled fantastic.

"Roddy, whatever that is, save me a plate!"

She grabbed a biscuit from the bread station and went to the grill, hoping for at least a little extra sauce, just to get a taste.

She needn't have worried. There was plenty to spare.

Rodrigo lay face down on his own grill. The flames were cranked all the way up, licking at the sizzling juices running down his bubbling, charred face. This close, the succulent scent of his roasted flesh was not just strong, it was the only thing she could smell.

Anna backed away from the grill. She looked another twenty years older than her fifty-eight years. The layers of foundation were powerless to stop her from going pale as winter. Every line in her face stood out like a dead riverbed. She wanted to scream. Her hands, warped into claws, pulled at her bottom jaw, opening it wider, the better to loose the scream swelling inside of her.

Except she couldn't get it out. She'd forgotten how to scream. She tried to remember but the only sound in her memory now was the crackling of Rodrigo's burning hair.

It was coming though. *I have no memory, but I must scream.* Must scream because the terror and revulsion was too much to be denied. It was chipping away at the block in her throat. She could feel it. Any second now she would scream.

The drops fell into her open mouth. Maybe half a shot's worth of hot copper.

Blood.

Anna looked up and Tony was there. The other waiter who'd gone to take a smoke break. He was pinned to the ceiling. Held there by butcher knives through his shoulders and knees.

Skewered. Bleeding. And worst of all, not dead. His hands were not impaled, and he reached towards her, even as more droplets of blood sprinkled her face.

"Run," he croaked.

Run. Not *help me.* Just *Run.*

Anna staggered back towards the door, helpless eyes still fixated on Tony. She still couldn't scream, but her feet worked adequately. She was going to get the hell out of there.

She hit something solid and cold. *The cooler. You're going the wrong way! Focus, Anna!* Yes. Focus. She needed to stop looking at what had already happened. She needed to pay attention to where she was.

But then she turned around and realized that she had not walked into the freezer.

She had walked into the largest of four… *things* that had somehow moved in to take up half of her kitchen without her even knowing it.

Anna stared. She knew in a split-second that these… *things* had massacred her staff. And as quickly as she realized this, she realized that she was too late to do anything.

Too late, even to scream.

-   -   -

The diner bustled on, unaware of anything going on in the kitchen. Silverware clinked against plates. Conversations continued on their normal path. Somebody asked if there was something burning in the back.

Then the kitchen door swung open and all other activities stopped. Not slowly. Instantaneously. The only sound, the only sound left in the entire world as far as any of them knew, was the heavy drumming the things from the kitchen made with every step. They did not tread carefully, these four. Their every footfall tolled thunderous and malevolent out into the empty silence.

The four approached the nearest table. They were aware that they commanded the focus of every eye in the diner, and the fear and awe they soaked in was more nourishing than the blood and meat staining their faces could ever be.

They came to the table where Marco, Marilyn, and Eric Hitch, those happy ramblers on their way back from the Grand Canyon sat. Just fifteen minutes ago, they had been on the highway somewhere east of here. While Eric napped in the back seat, Marco had squeezed his wife's knee and said, *"I know we'll have plenty of chances to try, but I'm not sure if we'll ever have a trip as good as this one was."*

That was then. Now Eric was trying to burrow into his mother's side. Marilyn folded her arms protectively around him. Marco held the butter knife that had come with the bread. He had it clenched tight in one white-knuckled hand and held it up in front of his face.

The four tried not to laugh.

They waited, but the moment did not end. A minute passed. The patrons may as well have been statues for all the life they showed.

As they often had to, the four took initiative. One of them stepped forward. Marilyn Hitch pulled her small son closer to her chest, but the thing from the kitchen did not lay a hand on him. All it did was set a serving tray down on the table.

Their waitresses' head stood upright on the tray in a sticky pool of her own blood. Like the patrons, her face was also frozen in its final rictus of terror.

For the first time since the four entered the diner, there was screaming then. Screaming and gurgling and the wet slap of blood flying everywhere.

Some of the patrons tried to run. A few even made it to the front door. A hulking trucker threw his bulk against the door again and again. More people piled behind him, pressing their weight against the cheap, hollow metal door, but no matter how many screaming, frantic bodies pushed against it, the door would not open.

That was because the four had taken care to twist a pipe handle around the front door before they came in through the back. The terrified crowd at the door could push all they want, but all they'd really done was set themselves aside for last as the rest of the diner patrons were ripped to bloody shreds.

Finally, their order too was up.

7

When Jack woke up, it had already gotten warm enough inside of the car for condensation to pool on the windows. A quick glance in the rearview mirror told him Luke was still curled up snoring in the back seat. His blonde hair was tumbled in a wave. He cradled the empty bourbon bottle like a lover in his arms. Which was fitting. Jack may not have gotten Luke laid yet, but the bourbon had definitely fucked him.

For his part, Jack felt fine. Careful not to wake Luke, he eased the door open and got out of the car. There was some stiffness in his knees, but all in all nothing too bad. This was not his first time sleeping in a car.

Luke's detour had taken them to a gravel parking circle at the mouth of a hiking trail. They decided to stop there for a little. Then Luke produced the bottle of Bakers he'd brought in his suitcase. After that, driving anywhere didn't seem like such a good idea.

In the morning light, it was hard to fault their judgment. The wind was already up, screaming its hushed secrets past his ears. Yucca trees dotted the golden landscape in front of him. Some of them must have been at least fifty years old- tall, twisted things with gnarled limbs. Trunks scarred by God knows what hardships.

But still here. The toughest place just to survive on the whole damn planet, and somehow they're thriving, Jack thought.

And then there was the hawk.

The raptor was perched up high in one of the tree limbs. It had the remains of its breakfast, some jack rabbit that hadn't been quick enough on the draw, strung over the same branch. The hawk knew Jack was there. Its flat, black and gold eyes bored right through him. It could have flown away if it wanted to, but the hawk just dipped down and ripped some organ loose from the rabbit's open ribcage. Whatever it saw in Jack, it didn't seem to mind his company.

From where Jack stood, he could see into the side view mirror. He glanced down at his own reflection, looked into his own eyes, and tried to gauge what he saw staring back at him.

Not the hawk. Not yet, at least. But he didn't see the puppy either. He looked into the dirty, clouded glass of the Firebird's mirror and saw no trace of the stranger that had stared back at him from the glass guitar case. That person had the eyes of an abandoned dog. A rag-eared mutt with pained, desolate eyes that belonged in a Sarah McLachlan commercial.

The person staring back at him from the Pontiac's mirror looked a little more like himself. A little stronger. A little more like a survivor. A little more defiant.

Jack leaned against the side of the car and closed his eyes. The heat of the sun was on his face and the wind was in his ears. He didn't need to see anymore, he just… *was.* And it was alright, for that moment, to just *be.*

And then a door slammed.

"Ah," Luke moaned. "Fucking SHIT!"

Jack opened his eyes. The hawk was gone. Luke was there, pacing back and forth and shaking the stiffness from his limbs.

"Son of a bitch," he hissed. He staggered to Jack's side on rigid, Frankenstein legs and then cracked his back with the pop of a dozen packing bubbles. "Jesus, if we crash in the car again, do me a favor and break my fucking legs off first." He cracked his neck and finally noticed the array of brown earth and blue sky spread out before him.

"Pretty," Luke remarked.

Jack sighed.

-   -   -

They stopped at a general store as soon as they hit a main road. Not a convenience store, not a CVS or a Rite-Aid; it was a squat, stucco structure with a screen door and dust permanently clinging to the windows. Inside, they grabbed the road version of breakfast and lunch- chocolate milk and saran-wrapped pastries for the morning, energy drinks and beef jerky for the afternoon. Luke doubled down on aspirin and bottled water to go with it. They fell into line behind a trucker who wore flannel and a quilted vest despite the heat. There was only one cashier, a Native American in his late fifties. Old, broad, and solid. Black hair with streaks of gray hung around his weathered, tired face like curtains around a window in an abandoned house. Luke nudged Jack in the side and nodded past the trucker's broad shoulder. "Check that out," he said.

Jack followed his gaze past the trucker and over the cashier's head. There was a mobile hanging there, slowly rotating in the lazy breeze from the fan. It was made from crisscrossed branches and rawhide strips. A charm dangled from the tip of each branch. It took Jack a moment to place what they were, but he eventually got it. There was a preserved bear's paw on one branch and a mountain lion's paw on the other, differentiated by size, color, and by the wicked curves of the cougar's claws as opposed to the broader, straight points of the bear claw. These were counter balanced by a mummified baby alligator head with its flat, green eyes spinning lazily at the end of its thread and, last of all, a set of shark's jaws large enough to sit atop the man's head like a crown of thorns.

That's what the old Indian had circling over his head morning, noon, and night. Bear, Cougar, Alligator, and Shark.

"What do you suppose that means?" Luke asked.

"That means the Peyote around here is fucking amazing," Jack murmured.

"No shit?" Luke stepped up eagerly as the trucker paid and went on his way. He placed his purchases on the counter and leaned in close to the cashier. "I'll take these… and some *special* snacks if you've got any." His eyes flicked suggestively to the mobile of animal parts overhead.

Jesus Christ, Luke. Jack thought. But if the Native behind the counter was offended, he didn't show it. "Sixteen seventy-four," was all he said.

Luke shrugged. *Can't shoot me for trying.* He took a twenty from his wallet.

The cashier didn't take it. Instead, he reached up and pushed back the thick sheets of his hair.

Luke gasped. Jack, naturally less inclined to outward reactions, didn't flinch, but his heart seized up and then resumed beating at a jerky, hectic pace.

The cashier's ears were nothing but ragged edged holes in the sides of his head. The flesh of his cheeks and head was ravaged by long gashes and deep divots as ragged as the landscape outside. His face was untouched, but the rest of his head was a wreath of scar tissue.

Claw marks, Jack realized. *Claw marks and bite marks.* Jack had been raised in a small town deep in the foothills. He knew a kid or two with similar marks. Never anyone as badly as what he saw in front of him, but he knew what they meant. *Once upon a time a coyote or something got after this poor bastard. Looks like it damn near got all of him too.*

A coyote. Or something.

Perhaps a bear or a mountain lion.

The cashier grinned. "Sixteen seventy-four," he repeated.

- - -

They left the store, the desert sun no longer quite as hot after the chill inside. "You had to ask, didn't you?" Jack said.

"I asked if he had drugs. I didn't say, 'Excuse me, friend, is your face a fucking nightmare hellscape? If so, would you mind if I had a peek?'"

"You're plenty polite when you're having luncheons with albino, neo-pagan sapiosexuals. It wouldn't kill you to show a little respect to the people out here too."

"I have to be polite because if I'm not they'll crucify me for it on Twitter. You think that guy fucking tweets?"

Luke's phone rang before Jack could respond.

"Hello?"

"Luke?" the voice on the other end of the phone said. Luke didn't recognize it, but it was female and pleasantly smokey and that was good enough to keep him on the line.

"Speaking," he said.

"This is Tricia Masterson."

"Well Tricia, what can I do for you? Professionally or personally?"

She sighed. It was oddly familiar.

"My maiden name's Galindo. I'm Jack's sister."

"Ohhhh, JACK'S sister," Luke said. He drew out the words to make sure that Jack caught them. "How'd you get this number?"

"You gave it to me at Jack's last album party. After I told you I was married."

"Heh. That does sound like me."

That sigh again. "Is he with you? I called him like a thousand times and he's not picking up."

"With me?" Luke asked. Jack waved him off emphatically. *"I'm not here,"* he mouthed.

"I haven't seen him, Trish. He was talking about going out to see Alice Cooper. They're probably out on a golf course somewhere, and you know how reception-"

"Put him on the phone, Luke."

Luke tossed the phone to Jack like they were playing hot potato. He met Jack's glare with a resigned shrug.

"Women yell, I listen. I blame my mother."

Reluctantly, Jack put the phone to his ear.

"Hey, Trish."

"Seriously? I have to hear about your life from freaking TMZ?"

"Did you want to see it on my Facebook page?"

"CALL. Asshole."

He rolled his eyes. "You done?"

In a kitchen in the South Bay, Tricia Galindo-Masterson switched the phone from one shoulder to the other. Her personality shifted with it. "Yes," she said. "Now tell me how you're doing."

I'm okay. Just two words. He'd said them so many times already that they should have come out as practiced and automatic as any other song he'd performed over the last ten years. But he tried to say it to his big sister, "*I'm okay,*" and the words simply would not come. All that escaped his throat was a mangled croak.

It was answer enough for Tricia. "Talk to me, Jack. No reporters, no fans, just me."

And he might have. At the very least he might have, for the first time in weeks, said Tracy's name out loud.

But that was when a high, excited voice cut in. "Is that Uncle Jack?"

The little girl was nimble. She pulled herself up onto the countertop and plucked the phone from her mother's hands with the same easy grace.

"Hi, Uncle Jack!"

Jack smiled. "Hey, Lucy. Still loopy?"

The seven-year-old sat down on the countertop. Drummed her legs against the dishwasher. "Guess what chord I learned today."

"Which one?"

"G!"

"G!?" Jack exclaimed. "Well, I'll tell you what. If you learn a D chord by this summer, I'll take you on tour with me for a week. How does that sound?"

"Absolutely not!" his sister's voice blared over the line. "Lucy, stop kicking the dishwasher and give me back the phone."

"I gotta go now," Lucy said. "Bye, Uncle Jack."

"Bye, kiddo."

Tricia took the phone back, but she already knew that whatever moment she had with her little brother was gone. She bit her lip. "Listen, Jack," she said. "Just be alright, ok? Not even good. Just alright."

"I will be," he said. "I am. Really."

I'd like to see you say that when I could look you in the eye, Trish thought. "And come by if you want," she said. "There's always room."

"Even if I bring Luke?"

"There's room for him in the garage."

Jack laughed, but heard nothing else from the other end of the line. She'd hung up.

Same old Trish.

Same old Jack? He wondered. He looked at the Firebird waiting for them in the gravel parking lot. He tried to imagine actually dropping by his sister's place in Redondo. Picking Lucy up and teaching her the intro to *Bark at the Moon.*

…No, not the same old Jack. Not yet.

8

Outside of Beatty, Nevada, they stopped at an actual bar. The sign promised live music, but the lead singer was also the local livestock veterinarian and the show wound up getting canceled because some rancher's horse broke a leg. Jack and Luke already had their beers when the cancelation was announced. Rather than lose their money, the most reasonable thing to do seemed to be to order shots. Judging by the noise around them, the rest of the patrons seemed to be similarly fiscally responsible. It was standing at the crowded bar, two different elbows jutting into his side, that something occurred to Jack.

"I'm surprised nobody's recognized me," he said.

"What's to recognize?" Luke asked.

"Tattoos. Head shape. The makeup doesn't cover that much, you know that."

Luke laughed. "You think that's how people can tell you're the guy under the skull? Jackie Galindo isn't your ink and your hat size, Jack. It's the sneer and the glare and the high concentration of 'fuck-you, motherfucker' that radiates from your every bone. You think someone's going to recognize you right now?" Luke shook his head. "I say again, what's there to recognize?"

Jack bristled. "This is me, Luke."

"Well it sure as hell isn't, Jackie."

"Is that what you're here for?" Jack challenged. "Did you come along to try and coax your meal ticket back out?"

"I came along to try and get you out of this tailspin. I'm trying to coax you back to your real life. The one where the greatest city on earth is full of beautiful women who would kill somebody for a chance to fuck you. I liked Tracy, I did, but you were together for three years. You were Jackie Galindo a lot fucking longer than that. For your own sake, you've got to go back."

"Yeah? Go back to what?"

"I don't know, how about Jane Jackson? She was always dropping hints about a threesome with you and Tracy. I'm sure she'd be satisfied with the one man show."

"Jane Jackson. Great. What else you got for me?" Jack asked. "A wedding? Kids?" His voice rose. "How about a fucking future? Tracy wasn't there for photo ops, Luke. She wasn't a goddamn stage dressing. I loved her. I wanted to marry her and every time I remember that she's not coming back, it makes me wish I was anyone except Jack or Jackie Galindo. So you tell me, what else can you line up for me? Because before I turn around I'm going to need to know that there's a lot more waiting for me than the same worthless shit I left behind."

He took his half-empty pint glass and slammed it down on the bar top. Beer splashed everywhere. "I knew you were just waiting to say something like this. I knew it, and that's why I didn't want you coming along. Because you grew up in too much of a fucking bubble to know what this feels like!"

It might have been true, but that didn't mean it was fair. And Jack regretted it the moment he said it. Luke stayed rigidly perched on his stool. He didn't reach for a napkin, even as Jack's spilled beer soaked deeper into his $200 jeans.

"I see your point, Jack." He said, voice stiff as his posture. "I'm sorry if I'm getting in the way of your 'Back to Welfare' experience. I wasn't trying to be a burden."

"Come on, Luke."

"Forget it," he said in that same formal tone. "Whatever you're going to say, I won't have the shitkicker background to appreciate it." He finally did dab at the stain on his pants and then raised a hand. "Bartender! Vodka-soda and a white wine over here!" While he waited for the drinks, Luke peeled a fifty from his wallet and left it on the table. "That's for this round and your next. Apparently I haven't done anything else for you over the last ten years, so the least I can do is pick up your tab." The drinks arrived. Luke picked them up and nodded towards a blonde sitting at a table by herself.

"I'll tell you what, Jack. I'm going to see if I can get that girl over there to give me a blowjob before she tells me her name. Don't worry, when I'm done I'll know where to find you. Still on this fucking stool."

Jack tried again. "Luke, don't-"

"No offense, Jack. Or maybe some offense, but I don't think you're qualified to give anybody any advice. Give me a call if you ever get back to LA."

And then Luke turned and focused his attention on the blonde. She looked to be about 25 and fit as all hell. She wore a flowered headband and a form-fitting maxi dress. Hippie for sure, either heading to or back from Joshua Tree probably. That was fine, Luke liked hippies. "Progressive" morals, no underwear.

"Hi," Luke said. He set the wine down in front of her and took a seat at the opposite turn of the round table.

The blonde didn't say a word. She looked coolly from the drink to Luke. Coolly, but not without some interest. "You take a real chance bringing a girl anything but beer or whiskey around here," she said.

Luke smirked back, trying to project amusement and just a little arrogance. "I've found you can't get anywhere in life without taking a risk or two." He leaned in. "How did this one pan out?"

She only shook her head and smiled. Luke wasn't complaining. There's something magical that happens when a beautiful woman smiles and shakes her head. It calls special attention to hair, eyes, lips, and, in this case, teeth. Even in the low light of the bar, Luke noticed she had very nice, white, even teeth.

"I'm guessing you're not a local," she said.

"What gave me away?"

"Not enough dirt on your hands."

"No dirt, but plenty of blood. I'm a music agent in LA."

Another flash of interest in the blonde's blue eyes. Stronger this time. "What are you doing out here?" she asked. "Talent scouting?"

"Talent sitting," he replied. "Client of mine got dumped and he's taking it like one of the fifteen year olds that buy his albums. He's out here because he's not ready to handle it like an adult yet, and I'm along for the ride."

"Then shouldn't you be with him?"

Luke shrugged. "He's made it clear he could do with a little break from my company. I'd call it cabin fever except we've been sleeping in a car." He paused. "Front seat and back seat, just so there's no confusion."

She smiled again. Thinly veiled hunger looked out at him from inside her dazzling blue eyes.

"Good to know," she said.

God, the *heat* coming off of her. She wasn't doing anything except sitting there, but the primal energy coming off of her was almost more than he could take.

"I can't say I'm too upset, honestly," he said, settling in and finding his groove. "It's nice to have company that does something other than stare out the window looking like *this*." He mimicked the glum, faraway look Jack had had on his face ever since they left LA. That was good to get a laugh out of her. Just a little one, but progress was progress.

"I mean," he went on, "Don't get me wrong, I feel for the guy, but is it so terrible if I want to have a little fun? It's not like anybody's dead."

"Not yet," a voice said behind him.

A man's voice.

Not Jack's voice.

Luke turned around and discovered two men looming over his shoulder. He must have been extremely entranced by the blonde because he hadn't even noticed either of them until they were practically right on top of him. That was saying something because they were very hard guys to miss. One of them was so tall that planes would have a hard time missing him. Luke had met both Trace Adkins and Mick Fleetwood, and this guy had an easy two inches on both of them. His work boots had to be size 16, and he must have gotten his flannel shirt by beating Paul Bunyan and stripping it off his corpse. It was summer so there was no way to be sure, but the guy had probably given up on glove shopping and just wore oven mitts when it got cold.

His associate wasn't tall. Luke actually had a good couple inches on him. But those two inches didn't seem like such a big deal considering that the other guy had shoulders like two normal short guys standing next to each other. His t-shirt was sleeveless, making it all too easy to see that he also had biceps like someone had taken the muscles from two normal-sized men and squeezed them into one body.

Luke had no way to tell which one had spoken to him, but neither option seemed particularly appealing. Especially not with the way they were both looking at him.

"Gentlemen," Luke said quickly. "I didn't realize the lady was with friends."

"These are my brothers," the blonde said.

"That doesn't make me feel better," Luke said out of the corner of his mouth. He quickly downed the rest of his drink. "Well, that's my cue for a re-fill. I'll just be on my way."

The tall one stopped him with one cinder block-sized hand. He had a thick nest of hair and an unkempt beard. His eyes were dark, unreadable chunks of coal in that shroud of hair.

"Stick around," he said.

The one built like a highway divider was clean-shaven and short-haired. It was easier to see the plain aggression on his face as he stepped up into Luke's personal space. "Yeah," he said. He gave Luke a gentle push back towards his chair. A gentle push that nearly sent Luke flying across the top of the table. "Make yourself comfortable."

"Hehhh, I don't think that's possible."

Luke kept waiting for someone to break this up. In LA, this was as far as any bouncer would let a confrontation go.

Except you're not in LA. You're in Jack's precious cowboy country. He fumbled for his wallet. "I'm being rude," he stammered. "Let me offer you guys a drink. Two drinks."

A hand fell on his shoulder. It didn't belong to the skyscraper or the wrecking ball.

It was Jack. He stood directly at Luke's side, opposite the two brothers. Despite the height disparity between the two men, Jack found a way to look both of them in the eye.

"Is there a problem here?" he asked.

"Jack, you don't have to worry about this," Luke murmured.

"I'm not worried," Jackie said. "I'm just making conversation." His gaze never wavered from the two men in front of him. "…Well? It's a pretty simple question." He dropped his hand from Luke's shoulder and curled it into a loose fist. "Do we have a problem here?"

The two of them forgot Luke and crowded up towards Jackie. That was fine. Big guys loved to crowd in on people. Big guys loved to throw their size around and make a lot of intimidating faces.

Jackie Galindo liked to fight.

They muscled in closer still. Jackie decided this was as close as they were going to get. After this, they either de-escalated the situation or they were both leaving in an ambulance. Maybe Jackie would be along for the ride with them, but he would count that as a fair swap.

The tall one loomed over him. The shorter one stood close enough that

Jack could smell the reek of his body spray.

And then they both broke out laughing.

The tall one reached out and slapped Jackie's back. It hurt more than most people could punch, but there was no malice behind it.

"We're fucking with you!" he crowed. "Well, we were fucking with *him*." He pointed to Luke, who flinched on reflex.

The short, broad one slapped Jack's other shoulder, evening out the numbness spreading across his back. "Our sister can talk to anybody she wants," he added.

A woman slid between them with a clutch of drinks balanced across her hands. "And she wouldn't listen to you if you tried to tell her otherwise," the new arrival said. She was a brunette. Dressed appropriately for a bar in the middle of the desert, khaki skirt and a denim shirt rolled to the elbows and tied off just above the belly button, but she wore her dark hair in a neat bun and her black-rimmed glasses spoke to a greater sophistication. She leaned over to set the drinks down. It was hard not to notice the graceful curve of her back. "You'll have to be patient with them," she said. "Growing up they had to choose between building muscle and building a sense of humor, and I think it's obvious which route they took."

Jack shrugged, as much to get feeling back in his shoulders as anything else. "It's cool."

"No," the shorter one said, already pulling up two more chairs. "Come on, we were dicks. Let us get you guys a beer."

Jack hesitated. "I don't know."

Luke knew. Now that the crisis had passed, he was eager to start peace talks. He nominated the blonde for negotiations. "I could use another beer, Jack," he said.

The tall one's beard opened to make space for a smile of yellow teeth. "That settles it." He lumbered back towards the bar.

Luke took an open seat, next to the blonde of course. Still reluctant, Jack sat down as well. "So," Luke said to the brunette, "We've obviously met the brothers. That would make you…"

"The sister," she supplied.

Luke leaned towards Jack. "Dude. Sisters."

"What was that?" the blonde asked.

Luke straightened up. "Just thanking my bud here for having my back when it looked like things were about to get rough." He spoke quickly, but then he turned to look Jack in the eyes. "Really. Thanks," he said with deliberate slowness.

Jack waved him off. "I owed you."

Their new friend came back with two beers. Jack helped himself to one. Bringing it to his lips, he allowed himself to see their new companions without looking through the filter of what would be the best way to put two of them in the hospital.

The blonde woman had caught Luke's attention for obvious reasons. Not just because of her body, which was admittedly spectacular, but because everything about her, clothes, wavy beach hair, big, white smile, it all screamed west coast southern California. To Luke, she must have been actual water in the desert.

The tall guy was a different story. The beard was too wild and the flannel too well-worn to be a hipster affection. It put Jack in the mind of somewhere northern and cold. Montana, or maybe Michigan.

The other brother was still another polar opposite. Deeply tanned and impeccably coiffed. He reminded Jack of every asshole he'd seen whenever a tour took him through the South Beach area.

And then there was the brunette. With some effort, he ignored the bare stretch of skin above the waistband of her skirt and focused the glasses. He saw the "Versace" logo stamped into the frame. And then there was the way she held onto a sense of calm, assured poise even as she reclined on a wobbly chair in a bar with $3 beers. Jack couldn't shake the feeling that he was looking at some high priced New York City lawyer on a rare casual Friday.

It was funny. The four of them couldn't be more opposite, and yet it was impossible to look at them all grouped together and not immediately notice the family resemblance that tied them all together.

Just like it was impossible not to notice the playful glint in the brunette's eye and the small, amused smile twisting the corner of her mouth as she caught him looking at her.

Still, Jack sipped his beer and did his best not to see it.

9

Six empties became twelve. Twelve became thirty-six. Thirty-six turned into sixty.

Somewhere between six and sixty, the group of them turned into old friends. Jack's jaw ached from laughing more than he had in weeks; and there was no doubt in his mind that that had more to do with the people around him than the booze flowing through his veins.

"You really don't recognize him?" Luke asked. Grinning and red-faced, he gestured at Jack like a game show host showing off a new car. "Jackie Galindo?" He bit back a beer burp. "Come on. He's been on the cover of *Rolling Stone* so many times, they ought to rename it."

The big guy with the beard shrugged. "Sorry, but I wouldn't take it personally. I'm outside a lot, don't get to hear much music."

"Don't be sorry," Jackie said. "It's a refreshing change of pace."

"I know some of your songs though," the blonde said. "I won't live anyplace that isn't near a record store and a lot of them play your stuff for ambience."

"I don't know what that says about the ambience where you live," Jack said, but his comment was drowned out by a burst of laughter from Luke as he threw an arm around the blonde.

"A girl who has to live by a record store! I love it! You're going to be homeless in five years, but I love it!"

They all laughed together. Luke left his arm where it was across the blonde's shoulders and she didn't seem to mind. She leaned comfortably against him and intertwined her fingers with his.

He still didn't know any of their names. And they only knew his because Luke had tried to flex the rock star muscle. Names seemed unnecessary between them. The pair of two and group of four had interwoven together in a way that transcended the need for names.

Luke obviously felt it too. "You guys are so awesome," he said. "If my family was like yours, we'd all be living together *Full House* style. I don't know why you only see each other every couple of years.

"We're all over the place," the squat bruiser said. "It's hard to get together even as much as we do."

"But," his brother said, raising his bottle in the air, "When we do make it work, we sure as hell make up for lost time!"

His siblings raised their drinks to meet his. Jack and Luke joined in and didn't feel the least bit out of place. They chugged whatever they had left, and slammed their drinks down just as a bell tolled and tolled from somewhere behind the bar.

"No way!" The blonde protested. "No way that was last call!"

"I'm with her!" Luke quickly joined in. "There has to be someplace out here willing to make some more money."

There were no objections. Just a scramble for keys and a rain of bills scattered across the table to even up their tab before the six of them shifted towards the door, as off-balance and uncontrollable as a category four tornado.

The blonde grabbed Luke's arm as soon as they stepped out into the cool air of the desert night. "You're coming with me," she said. Her face was split open by a wide grin that Luke did his best to match as she led him away.

Jack walked back towards the Firebird. His hand was on the door handle when a different set of fingers touched upon his wrist. Only feather light, but her touch went deep nevertheless. Deep enough to reach things that had been hurt by such a light touch and recoiled on instinct.

"You want to ride with me, Jack?" The brunette asked. The moonlight refracted off her glasses. It made her eyes glow in the gloom of the unlit parking lot.

Jack shrugged. "I don't know if I should leave my car here."

Be more obvious, Jack. Seriously. A meth head wouldn't waste time stripping that piece of junk for parts.

The brunette didn't do herself the indignity of acting like that was a real reason. "If you're worried I drank too much, I swear I'm okay. I can even say the alphabet backwards if you want."

"I can't even do that sober," he muttered.

She smiled in response and left it at that. No pressure, just an unlocked door. A door he could reach out and open. If he wanted to.

"Jackie!" Luke shouted, already far ahead of him and firmly wrapped in the blonde's control. "Think green! Carpool!"

The brunette was still quiet. Still patient. "It's okay if you don't want to," she said.

Part of him did. Part of him wanted to know what that dark hair looked like freed from its bun and flowing over her bare shoulders.

Part of him was still afraid to return to the same pool where he'd been hurt so badly before.

Part of him still felt loyal to Tracy.

But in front of him were those glowing eyes. And the warmth of her fingers at his wrist was like a homing signal in the cold of the desert night.

"Where are you parked?" he asked.

She nodded off in the direction Luke and the others were heading. There were only four cars there, parked all in a row at the far end of the lot. All four of them painted the same flat black.

A Dodge Ram, an Escalade, a Porsche, and-

"Mustang's mine," she said.

10

The convoy hurtled down Route 95 in a straight line. The Porsche was in the lead, followed by the Mustang and then the two trucks. The speed limit here was always a joke, but it was a particularly good joke at 3 o'clock in the morning. The group of them pushed the speedometers well past 90 without anyone raising a complaint except for the desert tortoises.

Jack and the brunette sat in silence. After three comfortable years with Tracy, small talk was like a foreign language that he'd learned once and had since completely forgotten. The girl didn't seem to mind, but how did he really know that for sure? He remembered as much about reading a woman's body language as he did about small talk. For all he knew, she'd already decided that he was a mute weirdo and couldn't wait to kick him out of her car.

Then she laughed. "Uh, oh."

Jack snapped out of his own head just in time to see the Porsche suddenly veer towards an off ramp. The others did not follow, continuing along the interstate and leaving the Porsche and its occupants to their own solitary adventures.

"I don't know if you noticed," the brunette said, "But I think my sister likes your friend."

"I just hope you guys have phones, because I know for a fact his is sitting in a cup holder back in the Firebird."

"You don't have yours?"

Jack looked out the window. "I felt like disconnecting for a while."

"…My sister told me what you're doing out here. I thought you big rock stars were the ones that did the heart breaking, not the other way around."

"I'm not a rock star," Jack said. "I'm just a guy who likes to play guitar and got lucky with a couple of songs." He turned his gaze towards the window. "My heart gets broken just fine," he muttered.

The brunette winced. "That came out kind of bitchy, didn't it?"

"How exactly did you think it was going to come out?"

"I don't know. Playful. Maybe a little bit flirty?"

"Well, don't sweat it. The way I'm feeling, bitchy works better for me than flirty."

They drove on with nothing between them but the buzz of wheels over asphalt.

"And maybe that's your problem," East said.

She jerked the wheel to the side and slammed on the brakes. The Mustang shot onto the dirt shoulder of the highway and went from ninety to zero in five seconds of flying dust, howling rubber, and grinding rock.

The pickup and the Escalade motored on, supremely unconcerned by the Mustang's sudden halt.

"Jesus shit fuck!" Jack screamed. The seatbelt pressed tight across his chest. He braced himself against the dashboard and the door and didn't relax until the car finally came to a stop. The dust cloud swirled so thickly around them, the headlights couldn't even pierce its brown haze.

The girl got out before the dust had even settled. Unthinking, Jack got out after her and slammed the door behind him.

They met in front of the car. "What the fuck was that!?" Jack yelled.

"I'm trying to get you to stop picking at scar tissue," she said. The brunette grabbed his face and twisted his head with surprising strength. She turned his gaze away from the road. Beyond the short, wire fencing, there was only ground empty of everything except for dirt and scrub brush. Sky empty of everything except ice-chip stars on the far side of space.

Beyond that emptiness, somewhere out there in the dark, almost as far as the stars, was Los Angeles.

And Tracy.

"Your pain," she said, "Is miles and miles of lifeless desert away from us. Nothing survives that trip unless someone's keeping it alive."

She turned his face back towards hers. It wasn't reflected moonlight now, but her eyes glowed nevertheless.

"Let. It. Die," she said. She sat up on the hood of the Mustang. She had to hike her skirt up to do it. Her bare thigh called out to him, beckoning him to follow as it disappeared into the shadows beneath the fabric.

"And fuck me."

She pulled him in by his belt and tucked him firmly into the open funnel of her legs. Jack allowed her to draw him in, but he resisted leaning in any further. Undeterred, she leaned in and kissed his neck. Her lips were as light as the slightest breeze. He might not even have noticed if he wasn't paying attention.

But God, he was paying attention.

"Your brothers-" he began.

"My brothers don't care," she said. She kept kissing him.

He tried again. "We're in the middle of the road."

Her lips moved up to his jaw. Her tongue ran along the curve of his chin. "We're to the side of the road."

His hands were at the small of her back. When had that happened? He pulled her in close. He felt the thin material of her shirt, and beneath that he felt nothing but the soft cushion of her breasts.

One last try. "I don't even know your name."

She moved higher still. Her lips brushed against his.

"East."

"East?" As a natural consequence, his lips had to brush against hers if he wanted to speak. "Is your sister West?"

"Mhm. And my brothers are North and South."

Her legs sprung closed like a pincer trap.

"But if it's alright with you, I'd really like to stop talking about them."

Her fingers were in his scalp now. Her eyes had captured his, as surely as if she'd snared fish hooks through his pupils.

But there was still one more thing that had to be said.

"I'm not-"

"Yes," she cut him off, "You are."

She pressed his lips to hers. No brushing this time, she hit him with a freight train of a kiss that rocked his brain to the back of his skull.

And Jackie took her best shot and came back hungry for more. He kissed her back and she moaned into it. He pushed her further up onto the hood of the Mustang and clamored up after her. She met him with her nails, working them under his shirt and marking his chest with delicious agony.

Jackie responded by diving down and biting her neck. East felt his teeth and *growled* at the sensation. He nipped and sucked at her warm skin, drowning in her and mad for more.

And, blissfully, East was all he thought of.

11

South followed his brother into the parking lot of a convenience store. The store stood alongside a laundromat, a used bookstore, and miles of absolutely nothing else. Its lights were the only lights to be seen in any direction, and the skinny dropout behind the counter was the only living person in sight.

Except for North and South.

South shifted the Escalade into park and stepped out. A gust of wind broadsided him. It made South shiver and scowl. He liked the desert fine during the day. At night, he hated it with every thin drop of blood in his body. Goose pimples crawled over his bare arms.

He hustled over to North's pickup truck. The tinted window was closed. From the other side of the glass, Steve Earle sang about The Devil's Right Hand.

South knocked on the glass, putting a little extra muscle behind it to make sure he could be heard over the music.

North turned down the music and rolled down the window.

At first glance, it seemed like North's beard had gotten shorter, but that was incorrect. His beard wasn't shrinking. It was *creeping* upwards. Thick brown hair climbed up North's face, crawling over his cheek bones and clustering around eyes that had turned as black as the truck's rumbling hood.

South grinned at the sight of his brother's creeping fur. As he did, his own eyes flooded with a dark green like rotting ferns.

-   -   -

Against the cold of the desert night, the Porsche windows had already fogged over completely.

"I know a spot," West had said. Except this wasn't a spot, this was just an off ramp that went off of everything. The road had just stopped and the desert had taken over.

That was where they were, and if they never left that suited Luke just fine. They were both completely naked inside of the Porsche. West on top with the sunroof open so Luke could see her bare body twist and writhe in all of its moon-lit glory.

The interior of the Boxster was cramped. Luke had the parking brake prodding dangerously close to his asshole, and West had one leg high over the passenger seat and the other one splayed behind her in a diagonal split.

But she made it work. Holy shit did she make it work.

"I didn't even think you could do this in a Porsche," he gasped as she ground her hips forward and mainlined another shot of delirium through his body. "You're a goddamn miracle worker."

Without missing a thrust, West bent down low, impossibly low, and licked his chest. "That's right, baby," she whispered. "I'm an angel."

"Oh, God," Luke moaned. "Whatever you are, just don't stop."

West obliged. She ground against him in a slow circle, keeping a hand flat against the window for balance.

Her hand had turned blue. The fingers had grown longer and rounder, like questing slugs. While she rocked and ground against Luke, her fingernails were turning bone white and slowly inching out into curved claws. The razor-edged tips screeched across the glass as they grew.

In his ecstasy, Luke noticed nothing.

12

Less than a half hour ago, Jack had lamented to himself how difficult it was to connect with another woman after spending three years with the same girl. It felt like having to relearn everything all over again.

However, as he and East groped and kissed and clutched at every inch of skin they could uncover, he discovered a serious upside to feeling like everything was new again.

Jackie had her shirt open. East's breasts were full and soft beneath his fingers; no implants, no underlying hardness, just perfect, natural flesh. East was just as ravenous. His body throbbed from the marks she'd scored into his flesh with her nails. He waited eagerly for more.

He kissed lower. Moving down her throat, over her collarbone, and towards the scented slope of her breast. The closer he got, the slower he went. He treated every new piece of flesh like a delicacy to be sipped and savored.

He was so absorbed in his samplings, he might have gone on forever without ever noticing the reflection of blue and red lights bouncing at them from the windshield. But the lights were one thing. The short *"whoop-whoop"* shout of the police siren was too intrusive to ignore.

"Uh oh," East murmured. Not that she made any move to pull his head away from her cleavage. "I think we're about to get a talking to."

"Relax," Jackie murmured against her warm skin. "I'm a rock star, remember?"

He turned around just in time to see the highway cop step out of his car. The man was older. Forties probably, inching towards overweight but not quite there yet. He certainly didn't walk like it. He didn't look at them with middle-aged eyes, either. His gaze was sharp and alert. *You two,* his eyes said, *Idiots like you at 3 in the morning are my bread and butter.*

"Evening, officer," Jackie said. "Good night so far?"

"Not as good as yours, I'd say."

East giggled and waved. She made no effort to close up her shirt.

The cop took in East's hills and plains, topography that would inspire the adoration of any man, and looked away with only minimal effort. "You mind making yourself decent for me, ma'am?"

Still laughing, East fled back into the shadows behind the car with her shirttails fluttering behind her.

"You too, son."

Grinning sheepishly, Jack buckled his pants.

"Guess you got a ticket for me."

"Even better, I've got an all-expenses paid trip for two at a *very* exclusive bed and breakfast. Afraid you're going to have a chaperone, though."

"Listen, officer," Jackie said. "I don't know if you recognize me, but if you've got kids I'm sure they do. I might even be up on their walls."

"I recognize you just fine. You look a little different without the Halloween makeup, but I do have two boys and they're both very fond of your *Antichrist's Cookbook* album."

"Yeah, that's popular that one. But better they like that than *End of Authority*, am I right?"

The cop was not amused. "I suppose you're looking for some special treatment."

"No, sir, I'm not," Jack said. "But just think about this for a second. Tomorrow, if TMZ reports that I got busted for having sex on the hood of a Mustang Mach 1, my stock just goes up and your kids have one more bad example to follow. On the other hand, maybe you just give me some BS ticket, I pay it quietly, and my friend and I find someplace else to go. Someplace indoors."

The cop's lined face never changed its skeptical scowl, but Jack sensed a subtle shift somewhere inside of it. Maybe, just maybe, a shift towards consideration.

"I'm with a decent girl, officer. And if this turns into something, you know and I know that her stock's not going to go up."

"Let me see your IDs," the cop relented. "If nothing prior comes up, we'll talk."

The shadow hit him then. It flew past Jack's blindside with a spine-chilling shriek and slammed into the police officer. It hit him so hard and so fast, the cop was in the air before Jack had the time to be afraid.

It slammed the cop down hard on the hood of his own car. The shadow let out another horrible screech.

"Jesus Christ!" the cop screamed. He fumbled for his revolver. Not slow. He got the weapon up in a quick draw that was more than training, it was innate talent. A born shooting man's speed.

The shadow lashed out faster and tore his hand off at the wrist.

He screamed. The shadow snarled. Neither of them sounded human.

Then the shadow lashed back the other way. Across the cop's throat. Blood sprayed across the hood. It ran down over the headlights and sprayed across the windshield. A few drops landed on Jack's face.

Those few drops were enough. *That's not stage blood and that thing's not a performer on your payroll. It's real. This is really fucking happening.*

Jack ran for the Mustang. He threw himself into the driver's seat and locked the door.

KeyskeyswherearethefuckingKEYS!?

He looked in the ignition. He checked the visor and the cupholder. Stupidly, he slapped his own pockets.

Tap. Tap. Tap.

He looked up.

East smiled at him through the glass. Her eyes were yellow with snake slit pupils, and they glowed for real now in the darkness of the night.

She was drenched in blood from the crown of her hair all the way down to the smooth glass pane of her belly. The soaked, crimson rag of her shirt clung to her flanks.

In one gore-streaked hand, she dangled the keys to the Mustang.

13

East unlocked the driver's side door and Jack lunged over the center console into the passenger seat. His hand fumbled for the door. *Getout. Go. Gowhere. Doesntmatter. Runnow.*

The driver's side door opened first. East poured inside with oily, silent speed before Jack even realized the door had closed again.

She sat facing him, curled up with her legs on the seat. Her flat, yellow eyes surveyed Jack with a kind of careless attentiveness. Her posture was the same way. Loose, and yet wound up. Relaxed, but ready to spring at a moment's notice. *Go ahead and run if you like,* that posture said. *I'm comfortable like this, but not so comfortable that I couldn't get up and run your ass to ground without even having to breathe hard.*

"What…" Had he spoken? He couldn't tell over blood the pounding in his ears. He swallowed. "What are you?"

East licked the cop's blood off the back of her hand, wiping it clean with long, slow strokes. "Say I told you," she said. "Would it make sense? How much talking would it take for you to understand even a little bit of what you just saw?" She turned her hand over and lapped up a long streak of blood from the heel of her palm to the tip of her middle finger. She licked four more fingers clean and then moved on to her other hand. Jack still didn't have an answer for her.

"That's what I thought," East said. Both hands clean, she cranked the key. The Mustang responded with a throaty growl like the finely tuned machine it was. She unfolded those long legs and put them on the floor. Shifted into first and rumbled back onto the road.

Too quickly, the cop car disappeared into the distance and they were alone in the darkness of the night. East didn't even turn the headlights on, probably didn't need to with those glowing yellow eyes. The Mustang was as isolated as a pressurized submarine in the darkest depths of the ocean.

He had a song that went something like this- *Diana Take the Wheel.* Jackie Galindo and the Goddess of the Hunt, savage immortals hurtling down a highway of darkness.

She's got the map and the moonlight

I've got the guns and the whiskey

Diana take the wheel
Huntress take the wheel
I'm the shotgun that you need
Baby, I'm the monster that you crave.

"What are you going to do with me?" Jack asked. His voice cracked twice.

"Leave you at the next rest stop," East said. Jack's stomach almost unclenched.

"And leave a little more of you at the rest stop after that," she said. "And then some more at the next one. And the next one. They'll be finding pieces of you all the way to Las Vegas."

Jack barely heard a word that she said. He was too transfixed by what was happening to her hands. He tried not to believe it. *It's too dark to know anything for sure. You're scared and it's fucking with your mind.*

It wasn't. The dashboard lights gave off enough illumination. He could see her hands grasping the wheel. He could see her fingernails, painted red, but not with nail polish.

He could see yellow, razor-sharp points breaking through the skin at the cuticle of each finger. He could see them growing long and curved in the lamplight.

Growing into claws.

Jack's scalp tingled, the flesh crawling where his hair would have been standing up if he had any. His heart hammered in his chest. The heavy, racing thud of it physically rocked his ribcage. It felt like he was standing next to a nine-foot speaker while his drummer cut loose with a solo. Again. And again.

"Is that you?" East asked.

She can hear it! Oh, God, she hears my heart!

And then Jack realized he could hear it too.

Thud.

Thud.

It was not his heart.

It was coming from the trunk.

It came again.

Thud.

Thud.

East pulled back onto the shoulder of the road and shifted into park. She took the keys and stuffed them into her shirt pocket. Those luminous-piss eyes fell on him again as the drumming continued from the trunk.

She reached for him with those yellow claws. Jack tried to recoil back, but too slow. Far too slow. She was on him-

And all she did was run her clawed fingers in circles along his inner thigh.

Thud.

Thud.

"I like you, Jack. You're fun to play with. That's why it would be a real loss if you tried to run and I had to leave your legs and everything between them here on the side of the road."

She got out.

Her slow saunter towards the back of the car was a deliberate taunt. East saw him through the rear windshield, twisted all the way around in his seat, watching her move further and further away, psyching himself up to make a run for it.

She knew he wouldn't. They never did. "Jackie," for all his bad boy bluster, was no different. East strolled leisurely around to the trunk. She even stopped to pick a rock out of her shoe, and Jack was still right where she left him. Big, brown, baby-deer eyes watching her, waiting for a mythical opening that would never come. She winked at him before she lifted the trunk.

Jack waited. The moment the trunk went up, obstructing East's view into the Mustang, he made his move.

He dove down into the footwell underneath the steering wheel.

-   -   -

East put her hands on her hips and surveyed the thing inside of the trunk.

"If I wanted extra bass, I would have installed a subwoofer," she said.

Marco Hitch, the family patriarch whose only sin was stopping at the wrong diner on the way home from the

Grand Canyon, couldn't answer her. The duct tape wrapped around his mouth was too tight.

He shouldn't have been able to bang on the trunk either. She noticed the crumpled strand of duct tape in one corner of the trunk. Obviously, she hadn't taken enough care when she was binding his hands and feet together. He tried to sit up, reeking of sweat, terror, and his own waste. East shoved him carelessly back into the trunk.

-    -   -

Jack ripped the cover off from underneath the steering column and yanked out a tangle of wires.

Old car, old wiring. You can do this.

At least, he used to be able to do this. Back when he was 16 and he and his gearhead pals thought it was hilarious to boost each other's beaters and hide them all over town. He didn't know if he could do it on the first try in the pitch black when he was twenty years out of practice.

You can. You can or you're dead.

He ran his fingers over the wires.
Step one, he needed something to
scrape the casings. He didn't even have
any change in his pockets. He dug into
the cup holders and felt nothing except
smooth plastic.

Fucked now, Jackie, some gleeful
voice insisted on declaring.

No. Jesus, no. He couldn't be stuck
already.

His earring!

He worked the scimitar piercing
from his cartilage and scraped the edge
over the wire casing. He began to work.

- - -

East reached for him. "I can think of
another way to keep you quiet," she
said.

Marco shrank away now, deeper
into the dubious safety of the trunk.
East found him anyway. One clawed
hand wrapped around his wrist. Marco
made panicked, frantic, pleading noises
from behind his gag.

- - -

Whatever, *whoever*, was in the trunk, Jack heard it protest like a terrified piglet.

He worked more frantically with the wires.

- - -

East grinned at the man's muffled protests. Any louder, and he'd stretch his jaws until the tape ripped from his mouth. She'd seen it before, duct tape clinging to a man's chin, his upper lip raw and bloody because he'd ripped off most of his skin along with the tape. Just the thought of it made East's teeth elongate until the sharpened points crept past her bottom lip. Her ears itched, eager to migrate towards the top of her head. To continue the conversion.

Which came first? Did her appetite for cruelty encourage the change? Or did the change sharpen her hunger for suffering? Truthfully, she still didn't know. And it seemed less and less important as the shift continued and her Meat Mind fell further and further away.

-   -   -

Red wire and green wire. At least, in the dark, he hoped they were the red wire and the green wire. Red and green, that had been the combo on Frankie Vasquez's '83 Mustang. Same make and model. They had to be the same.

They were hopefully the same. How much longer could she stay back there doing… whatever she was doing? Not long.

Not long enough for a second try.

-   -   -

East looked down into the trunk. Her siblings would have pulled him apart by now. Only East savored the fear as much as the pain. That wide, double high beam stare darting back and forth between her eyes and the claws wrapped around his wrist. The high, frantic in and out of his breath and the muffled screams from behind the tape. *Knowing* that she was going to rip his hand off and *knowing* that there was nothing he could do to stop her.

117

The engine coughed then. *Her* engine. It sputtered to silence just as quickly, but did the Mustang just decide to turn on all by itself?

It most certainly did not.

-   -   -

Shit!

Jack scraped the ignition wires together again. The engine stuttered longer this time, but still didn't catch.

Jack tried one more time.

Please, you bitch. Giddy up. He scraped the wires together and was blessed with a full-throated roar from the Mustang. He twisted the wires together to keep it running and scrambled up into the driver's seat. He shifted into first and spared one look into the rearview mirror, just to see where East was.

He looked back at the same time East slammed the trunk down, just in time to catch the fucking *monster* reflected back at him.

The brake lights lit her face up in devil's red. East's nose had flattened and her ears had climbed up to the top of her head. A coat of thick fur covered her face and neck. Her teeth were the worst. Long, needle sharp, and twisted in a furious scowl.

And she saw him looking. Her eyes narrowed with hatred.

She screeched. A terrible, wild cat howl loud enough to drown out the engine. Jack slammed on the gas. The Mustang surged forward. The acceleration pushed Jack's body deeper into the seat.

And then his head slammed into the steering wheel as the car jerked to a halt just as quickly.

East had her curved claws buried in the chassis of the Mustang, holding it in place. Jack slammed on the gas again. 300 Horsepower straining to break free, and East reined it in with nothing but her bare hands. She was still transforming, becoming longer and more angular, her body rippling with extra muscle. The tires squealed and the car whipped from side to side. East snarled and kept it exactly where it was.

Jack slipped the transmission into neutral and then hard into reverse. The Mustang surged backwards, covering the arm's length between the bumper and East's chest in less than two seconds.

Less than two seconds was all her feline reflexes needed. East leapt up over the bumper and came down on the roof with a thud like a falling telephone pole.

Jack screamed. He shifted into drive and slammed on the gas. Gravel flew as he blasted onto the road. He glanced into the rearview mirror, hoping to see East tumble off the back of the car.

Instead, the driver's side window exploded and four claws flashed at his face.

Jack flinched to the side. The slash that should have taken off half his face instead merely sliced off the bottom of an earlobe. Blood ran down his neck, and seeped hot and wet underneath his shirt.

He swerved back and forth, crossing the centerline again and again as he hurtled down the empty highway. Hopefully, East would be too busy holding on to slash at him again. He turned on the high beams and scanned the road ahead of him. If he had one hope, it was somewhere out there. Hopefully just past the horizon.

If it wasn't, he had his bleeding ear to remind him what would happen next.

Crouched on the roof, wind whistling past her ears, East screeched her exhilaration into the night. The Mustang beneath her paws careened across the centerline again and then whiplashed back to the other side. East shifted easily with the move. Her center of gravity was completely unruffled by the 90 mile an hour maneuver, but her heart raced to keep pace with the eight engine cylinders hammering underneath the hood.

I'm going to kill you, little rock star, she thought. *Kill you and hang your eyeballs from my rearview mirror. But you're forcing me to kill you before I finished playing with you, and I can't even remember the last time anyone was that tricky.*

She reached down again with her cougar's claws. This time, she wasn't reaching for his face.

-   -   -

There! Bright, white light gleamed at the horizon. Small, distant, but unquestionably there. Jack felt no relief at the sight of them, only grim desperation like he was playing a bad hand of poker but was too deep into the pot to fold. He could die as well, probably would die as well, but he would get to see the last card come up. That was something.

He hurtled onward, devouring road. The off ramp came up and he took it at seventy miles an hour. The Mustang's chassis groaned against the torque wrenching at its frame.

He was close enough now that the light had taken on shape. Three rows of gas pumps and a snack-mart situated in the middle of an empty parking lot. A rest stop.

"Final Resting Stop." Save that one for later.

Jack ignored the voice. He put it into fifth gear, and the Mustang opened up further. The service station loomed ever larger.

East's claws hooked into the driver's side window frame. Ripped the door off its hinges. Jack abandoned the wheel on instinct. He flung himself across the center console at the same time that the dark, snarling thing swung into the Mustang.

East yowled. She lunged. Jack kicked her in the face. He caught her in the snout but may as well have kicked a concrete wall for all the good it did.

He tumbled into the passenger seat. At the same time, his hand found the handle and shoved the door open. He threw himself headfirst from the car. The blurring road rushed up to meet him and Jack didn't close his eyes. The oncoming asphalt was his salvation.

A salvation he was denied. His free fall stopped short just as fresh pain flared up in his leg. He hung with his upper body dangling inches from the pavement.

East had him by the calf. Her claws were dug in high up, almost at his knee. She bunched up her muscles and dragged him back into the Mustang.

"No!" Jack screamed. He held onto the frame for dear life, knowing that there was no point. The flapping door battered his shoulders. His fingers were already giving way while the pain in his calf only burned hotter. There was no breaking free. It was pointless.

He held on anyway. Let her work for it if she wanted him.

East obliged. She pulled at Jack and put real power behind it. Enough power to easily peel his fingers loose and pull him back into her clutches.

It was too much power. Jack's calf gave way before his fingers did. East's claws ripped free from his flesh in a gout of blood and torn muscle. Jack felt the pressure on his leg suddenly disappear, and just like that he was free falling out of the car. Away from East.

And down to the asphalt. Jack careened across the pavement, skin peeling away with every fresh bump across the asphalt.

Inside the Mustang, East's claws ripped through the leather seat where Jack's ass had been just a second earlier. The passenger door still flapped in the breeze. She shrieked her frustration and coiled up to spring after him.

That was as far as she got before the thunder hit her. Before the hailstorm of broken glass pelted her flesh and the

scream of ripping metal drowned out
even her agonized howls.

14

"You're not supposed to move him."

"We're just going to take him inside."

"You don't know if his spine's broke. You want to put 'im in a wheelchair for life?" The voice posing this question had maybe been feminine once, but that was before many years of cigarettes and poor health had their way with it.

"You're supposed to keep him warm!" The responding voice persisted. It should have belonged to an adult male, but it had the petulant, whining timbre of a disagreeable toddler.

"That's if someone's in shock!"

"I think he's been shocked enough to qualify, Lori!"

Jack opened his eyes. The people arguing over him both screamed.

There were only two of them. A squat, heavy woman with close cropped gray hair, and a thin, reedy teenager with stringy hair and the regrettable beginnings of a goatee. Both of them wore red vests with nametags over the heart.

"Holy Moses!" the woman gasped.

The young man got over his surprise a little quicker. He crouched down beside Jack.

"Are you ok, man?"

"Don't move him, Ken!" the woman chastised.

"I'm not!" he shouted back.

Jack sat up on his own. That was about as far as he could get. His shirt was off and there was an open, and mostly empty, first aid kit by his hip. While he was unconscious, the two of them had bandaged him up as best they could. Gauze encircled his torso and clumped in pads at his shoulders and on his leg. They seemed to have stopped the bleeding, but there was nothing they could do for the pain gnawing throughout his body. Experimentally, he lifted his arm and was rewarded with fresh pain flaring up all along his right side.

"Easy," the woman cautioned. Her nametag read, *Lori*. "We called 911.

The police and an ambulance are on their way."

"You may also want to call your insurance provider," Ken put in. This earned him a caustic glare from Lori.

Jack ignored them. "Where is she?" he asked.

Ken and Lori exchanged a quick, anxious look.

"Was someone with you?" Ken asked. "We didn't see anybody else."

Not there. Jack's pulse tripled. His heart slammed against his aching ribs.

'She wasn't in the car?

He finally saw what was left of the Mustang. It was accordioned into the back wall of the snack mart, just like he'd planned. The Mustang was a complete wreck.

But she was supposed to be inside it.

He scrambled to his feet.

"Hey!" Ken shouted.

Jack pushed him away. He swung around in a circle. He saw the snack-mart. And he saw the gas pumps underneath their baseball stadium spotlights, but everything beyond their glare was darkness and emptiness.

Except that the darkness no longer seemed so empty.

"Oh, Lord," Lori gasped.

"What?" Ken asked.

"He's talking about the cat."

Jack whipped back towards her. "You saw it!?"

Sick with dread, Lori nodded.

"We didn't realize it was a pet," she said delicately. "When we saw the crash, and what it did to you… the scratches, we just figured…"

"*When Animals Attack*, man," Ken concluded. Lori elbowed him sharply in the ribs for his troubles.

Lori, who'd received a stitch or two from her seven shelter babies, maintained more sympathy.

"She's still there," Lori said gently. "If you need to take a moment."

Jack did need to take a moment, but not the kind that she thought. He slowly made his way towards the Mustang's final resting place. Every step he took came with a primal, crushing pain through out his entire body. It seemed like no one thing was broken, but every part of him was deeply, structurally cracked.

Jack's weary, plodding pace gave him plenty of time to marvel over the fact that his desperate, last gasp of a "plan" had actually worked. He hadn't really expected it to. First, he'd been worried he wasn't going to find anything to smash into before East could pry him out of the driver's seat. Then, he was certain that he'd taken his foot off the gas too far away to hit the back of the store with enough force. And even if he had been going fast enough, then he half-expected to smash his head open jumping out of the car.

The closer he got, the less certain he had became. Even if the cashiers said that his "pet" was inside, he didn't believe it.

The Mustang's interior was a crumpled soda can. He could see that much. She *had* to be dead. If she wasn't, she…. whatever she was, would be picking him out of her teeth right now, wouldn't she? There was no way she could have survived that. Nothing could.

He drew closer. He didn't see anything moving in the dark confines of the Mustang, but he was prepared to fling himself back the second he needed to.

…He didn't need to.

East was still in the driver's seat.

East was never going to leave the driver's seat.

Upon impact with the rock, the Mustang's engine had torn loose and pistoned directly into the driver's seat. The 500-pound fist of metal hadn't just hit East, it had turned her legs into pulled pork and practically snapped her spine in two. She was bent over backwards. Twisted so far back that her face was staring up at the ceiling. There was no glowing yellow fury in her eyes now. There was only flat, lifeless amber. Her cougar's face still wore its final, terrible sneer, but it was the frozen sneer of a taxidermy display.

She was dead.

The moment Jack accepted, truly accepted, that East was dead, the floodgates cracked open. Whatever pain he felt, there was more of it, torrents of it, held back and hidden because his need to survive had kept it at bay. Knowing that she was truly gone, the full weight of his pain hit him. He had to lean against the ruins of the Mustang just to stay standing. Pain replaced everything. Agony closed around him like hands cupped around a captured moth.

And Jack welcomed it. *It's okay,* was what the pain really meant. *It's fine if you're exhausted. You're allowed to feel ripped up, stomped down, inside-out and then turned outside-in again. It's all right if you're pissing-your-pants terrified. You won. You're walking away, and she's fit to be turned into guitar strings. You're allowed to feel whatever you want.*

A warm, clammy hand pierced through the pain and settled on his shoulder.

"We always love them, don't we?" Lori said. She sniffed back a tear. "Even when nobody else can understand why." Her doughy, deeply trenched face was stamped with such sincere compassion, Jack couldn't bring himself to tell her the truth.

Save it for the cops. Them and Luke are the only ones that need to know the whole story. Whatever the hell the whole story actually is.

And then it hit him.

LUKE!

If East had been… whatever the fuck she was, then what the hell did that make West?

"I need a phone," he said to Lori. "I need one NOW."

'It's okay," Lori assured him. "An ambulance is already coming."

Jack grabbed her vest. "Listen to me. I need a fucking phone. My friend's in trouble."

Ken barely heard any of this. He'd subtly slipped out his own phone and turned it towards the ruins of the Mustang. This was the craziest thing that had ever happened in his eight months working at the Shell station. No way he wasn't going to get some pics. Maybe he could even sell a few to Buzzfeed or Gizmodo or some shit.

Ken got the camera app on and waited for the focus to sharpen. He heard raised voices behind him, but he ignored them. Just Lard-y Lori and the Crazy Cat Guy wailing over the dearly departed fuzzball.

He zoomed in, right on the mountain lion's frozen, fucked-up face and grabbed a shot. He pulled out a little bit, getting a nice wide angle of the thing all jacked up in the driver's seat.

He snapped the second picture just in time to capture the blur of the Cougar's claws lashing out at his face.

Ken's screams seized their attention. Jack and Lori whipped around and stood transfixed, watching Ken shriek and shudder with hooked claws in his eye sockets and blood gushing over the asphalt at his feet.

He screamed one more time. Time enough for Lori to realize exactly what was happening.

And then the Cougar ripped Ken's face off in a spray of blood and broken bone.

Lori wailed. Ken didn't collapse right away. He swayed there on his feet, the Ken she'd always thought of as *her* Ken, even though she was twice his age and twice his size. The Ken whose face was now little more than red slush with hair and a chin.

The Ken who fell, never to get up again.

Jack noticed none of this. He only had eyes for East. The Mountain Lion wrenched the door off its frame. Its baleful yellow eyes stayed fixed on Jack the entire time. The Cougar yowled and gnashed at him with broken teeth.

Jack stumbled back. He turned to run as a sound like rupturing packing bubbles crackled behind him.

That sound was East's vertebrates fracturing as it left its hind legs for a lost cause. East, pulling away from the engine block that had its bottom half pinned in place. The Mountain Lion did this without a second thought or even a first thought. Any hint of a Human Meat Mind was gone. There was only the Cougar's fury and pain, and its sole target was Jack Galindo.

15

Jack couldn't run. Even with East shrieking at his heels, the best his broken body could muster was a shuffling limp. He looked over his shoulder.

East trailed only a few feet behind him. The Mountain Lion's legs were gone, a long, red trail marked its path away from the Mustang, but it clawed its way across the asphalt at an unrelenting pace.

Jack shuffled faster. His calf wound opened back up. Hot blood ran down his leg and left a spit-spot path behind him. The scent of it drove East into a greater frenzy. It hauled itself along faster after him.

Jack reached the gas pumps at the exact moment he couldn't take another step. He pitched forward and clung to the pump to stay upright. He dug into his pocket, realizing only now that he wasn't even sure he still had his wallet.

Left pocket first. Empty. He went into his right. Nothing.

He slapped both back pockets. There! He felt the bulge against his left cheek and ripped his wallet out.

Somewhere, not too far behind him, East yowled again. The sound scraped like sandpaper through his head.

Jack pulled out a credit card and let the wallet slip from his shaking fingers. He dipped the card into the pump's card reader.

Credit or Debit?

Credit. He slammed on the button with all his weight.

Enter Zip Code

90068.

ENTER.

The lights running over the hoses flashed. Regular. Premium. Super Premium.

Driven by some mad instinct, Jack selected Super Premium. He drew the nozzle from its holster at the same instant that claws dug into his thighs and yanked his legs out from under him. Jack fell. The gas pump came loose from his hand.

He rolled over and those noxious yellow eyes and dirty fangs filled his vision. Jack got his arm up at the last second and shoved it into East's throat. The Cougar shrieked and snapped at the air inches from his nose. Bloody froth dripped from East's mouth and trickled down Jack's face.

Jack strained to hold the creature back. Even missing half its body, the wild cat was impossibly strong. He braced his wrist with his free hand, but his elbow was already folding inwards.

No. No, no, no.

Jack tried to squirm loose but the Cougar's claws sunk into his shoulders and held him in place. It pinned him down like a mouse it was finally done playing with.

The tire iron whipped around the side of its head and struck East in the temple. The Mountain Lion's skull, already weakened from the crash, cracked and sent bone shards flying into its eye. East yowled and rolled off of Jack. The miserable screeching continued as it clutched the bleeding ruin of its eye.

Marco Hitch didn't miss a beat. He stumbled after East, tape strands dangling behind him, filthy with blood and sweat. He coughed up more blood.

He limped. His left arm looked broken but his right arm, the arm clutching the tire iron, seemed to be working fine. Marco brought the tire iron down again on the Mountain Lion's ribs and then struck it in the snout. East's nose *crunched* and gushed blood.

"Eric!" He screamed, and smashed East in the head again. The cat's skull didn't crunch, it *squelched.* "Marilyn!"

He hit East again. "Eric! Marilyn! Eric! Marilyn! I'm gonna kill you, you fucking bitch! *I'M GONNA KILL YOU!"*

Panting for breath, Jack tried to sit up and process what he was seeing. East was down, he understood that much, but who was the bloody wraith strafing it with a tire iron? Jack couldn't say for sure, but he suddenly had an idea of just what it was East had in the trunk.

It doesn't matter now. Jack groped for the gas nozzle.

Marco Hitch was, in fact, already dying. Had he known this, he would have been grateful to hear it. There was nothing left for him in this world. Nothing except stomping out this fucking monster writhing on the ground in front of him.

He reversed his hold on the tire iron and drove the blunt tip down deep under the fucker's rib cage. The Wild Cat screeched so loud, Marco hoped Eric and Marilyn could hear it up in heaven.

If not, he yanked the iron rod back out, *Let's see if they can hear it this time.* He brought the tire iron down again.

And East rose up and wrapped its arms around him. It almost could have been a hug. Its claws dug into his kidneys. East *pulled* and twisted Marco Hitch open like a bottle of soda.

East pushed the gushing corpse aside. The Cougar was dying too, lifeblood gushing from a dozen different ruptures, but it couldn't die yet. The rockstar was still out there. East would find him. It would die with his meat in its throat.

The burning rain found her first. It came in a deluge, scalding her wounds and flooding her one good eye in fire. The scent of it clogged her nostrils and its torrential roar clogged her ears. East shrieked and writhed beneath the downpour.

Jack poured it on. He held the hose trigger in a deathgrip and doused the Mountain Lion in gasoline. The number on the pump ran higher and higher. Two gallons. Five. Nine.

When the Mountain Lion was completely drenched, Jack threw the nozzle at its face, a final impediment, and limped towards the minimart. He left East shrieking on the pavement behind him. The gasoline left it blind and writhing.

But no longer deaf to the receding beacon of his shuffling feet

And no longer so overwhelmed by that acrid scent of petroleum that it couldn't smell his blood.

East rolled onto its belly. It dug its claws into the asphalt and dragged its ruined body after the one who'd hurt it so.

16

Heart pounding, vision clouding, Jack reached the doors into the minimart. He grabbed at the handles, but the doors only rattled in place.

They were locked.

He slammed on the glass. "Let me in!" he screamed.

He could see what he needed inside. Right there on the counter, just behind the 5 Hour Energy shots.

A spinning display case of Zippo lighters inside of a Plexiglas box.

And beyond them, tucked behind a Good Humor cooler, a crescent curve of Lori the cashier's back and buttocks as she cowered out of sight.

"OPEN UP!" Jack screamed. "LET ME THE FUCK IN!"

The only answer was East snarling behind him.

Jack didn't ask again. He grabbed the cigarette butt container beside the door and swung it into the storefront window like a club. The safety glass spider-webbed on the first strike. The second smashed the glass apart and Jack stumbled into the store.

He made it to the zippo case. He saw the keyhole in the knob and didn't even bother to check if it was locked. He swept the display case off of the counter. It struck the floor and actually bounced. Didn't break. Didn't even crack.

"FUCK!" Jack screamed. He dropped to his knees and slammed the case with both fists but the Plexiglas didn't even tremor. He swung around in desperation for his ash can club.

What he saw instead was East crawling through broken glass. Still coming for him. One yellow eye was a mess of blood-clotted fur and swollen tissue. The other had turned an ugly orange shade, a flickering flame that still burned hot, even on the verge of going out.

Jack abandoned the lighter case. He lost his balance and stumbled backwards. On his knees, he crawled out of sight.

East's good eye was cracked open in a narrow slit. It saw him disappear behind a rack of chips and followed behind him. It didn't even spare a glance for the Fat Meat squealing and scrambling for cover. It was *him* East wanted. Only him. It clawed around the corner.

And Jackie was waiting for it. He had a can of air freshener clasped in one hand. He had a lit BBQ lighter in the other.

He triggered a blast from the spray can. The aerosol immediately blossomed into a foot-long burst of fire. The Cougar was maybe a little further away than that, but it was close enough. East went up in flames.

The Cougar howled. Screeched. Rolled and writhed at his feet like a fish jumping out of water.

Or maybe like bacon sizzling in a pan.

Jack breathed in. Breathed out. This close to the Cougar's funeral pyre, the heat made his skin tighten.

Breathe in. Breathe out.

East burned, but didn't die. It just kept thrashing and screeching. The sound of it clawed at his ears and kept digging down. Somehow, it just kept getting louder.

Louder.

Jack couldn't take it anymore. He ran for the hole he'd smashed in the front window. East's dying wails filled his ears and he needed to be away from them more than he needed to be away from the creature itself.

Jack ran, the last of his courage left at the Cougar's burning feet. He burst through the glass and the shrieking was still there. So loud, Jack didn't even realize he'd been shot at until a bullet hole appeared in the glass door beside his head.

The cop who fired still had her gun leveled at Jack. She looked as terrified as Jack was. And she looked like she was very close to firing again before another officer knocked the barrel skyward.

"Put that down!" the older cop bellowed.

It didn't matter to Jack. He fell to his knees and slumped on his side, grateful for the cop's loud bellow. Grateful for all the cops in fact. There were four of them in total, and Jack was more grateful for each one than the last. Especially for the one that had shouted.

The guns and flashing lights were good,
but the shout was best of all.
The shout signified Authority.

17

North and South had posted up in the convenience store. They'd liberated tall boys from the cooler and they had their choice of chips from the rack.

Best of all, they still had the cashier. His mangled body fit neatly between them in the space they'd made for it. North plucked out one of the man's eyes and rolled it in crumpled potato chips for a little extra flavor. He popped it into his mouth and chewed.

South popped open another can of Miller. Set it beside North and then opened one for himself.

"West," South croaked. Jack and Luke would have not have recognized his voice. The voice they'd bonded with with over beer had transformed into a gurgling rasp, like the words had to crawl through a swamp of poisonous fumes to leave South's throat.

North drained his beer before answering. *"Leave her. They'll find us when they're done."* His voice was different too. It was huge. Too huge to come from even someone as big as him.

South shook his head.

"We should go West," he said. *"Tomorrow. California. Water."* South's eyes turned faraway and longing. *"Warmth."* It was more than the sound of his voice that had changed. It was the content. South spoke like someone losing command of the language.

North dug out the clerk's other eye. Rolled it in Doritos this time. He shrugged. *"Tell West."*

North waited. And grinned when South kept his chin tucked down. *"No?"* North prompted. He held up the clerk's other eye. *"Tell him?"*

South swatted the eyeball from his brother's hand.

North chuckled.

And then the thorns erupted inside his skull. North screamed and clutched his head. Black claws sprung from his fingertips and scoured his scalp, but he barely even felt them. They were nothing compared to the pain expanding inside his mind.

But that was wrong. The pain wasn't something extra, it was something absent. Part of him withering and dying but screaming and clawing for survival as it shriveled to nothing.

And he wasn't alone.

South was screaming too.

…When his senses finally returned, North looked around and discovered that he and South had demolished half of the store. They'd ripped the doors off the coolers, twisted display shelves to scrap. Light fixtures dangled down from the ruined ceiling, casting the convenience store in flickering shadows.

South lay crumpled on the floor. At some point, he must have rolled over the cashier's corpse; his body was slick with dead man's blood and his own tears. They were both panting, physically unharmed but spiritually ravaged. North was on his knees. Getting up seemed impossible. North couldn't figure out how he could ever face the world again with this gaping hole torn into his soul.

South found a way. Baby brother South. Last to run, last to talk, last to

Change, and now the first to find his will again. He stood up and clenched his hands into fists. Fists turning green and craggy as they tightened.

"He killed our sister," South said.

Just like that, North found a way to stand up again too.

"No," North said. The words were barely words. They tumbled out like mangled things from between teeth that were now fangs. *"He killed himself."*

18

West wasn't screaming. She was moaning as she rocked back and forth on top of Luke. Her eyes were closed, the better to enjoy the sweat coating her skin and the pleasurable, filling sensation that throbbed and pulsed inside of her. It felt good. Good enough to leave the Meat alive a little longer.

Then the wave hit her too and West opened her eyes.

They were jet-black.

She screamed. It emerged from her slim, tapered throat in a roar like a rusty boiler flaring to life. The sound of it snapped Luke from his ecstasy. He opened his eyes. He saw that the blonde's beautiful eyes had rotted black. He saw blood pouring from the screaming chasm of her mouth.

"Jesus fucking Christ!"

Teeth sprouted from West's bleeding gums. Dual rows of short, triangular points crowding her mouth until there was no room for any more.

And then, before Luke's unbelieving eyes, her mouth began to *grow* to make room for more teeth.

And the rest of her was growing along with her mouth. The petite, tight blonde wasn't so tight and petite anymore. Her body swelled and swelled until her mass took up almost the whole interior of the Porsche.

And, still, she was screaming. Growing louder and hoarser to match the rest of her body.

The tableau unfolding held no fascination, morbid or otherwise, for Luke. He'd seen enough. More than enough. While the blonde bellowed and her black-eyed face ballooned outwards, he flipped onto his belly and flung the door open. He fell out of the Porsche and scrambled up just as quickly. Bare-ass naked, Luke took off running into the night. Not caring where he was. Not caring where he was going. Away was the only thing that mattered.

For three seconds, this was the blissful world Luke got to inhabit. A world of nothing but his own breathing and the blood pumping in his ears.

And then that world ended in thunder. The thunder of something storming across the desert dirt.

Something chasing after him.

Luke kept running. Rocks and dead branches drew blood from his feet. He didn't care.

The thing behind him cared. It could smell every crimson drop.

Luke didn't dare look back. What he could hear was enough. First, the heavy pounding of feet. And now deep, bellowing breath. The feel of it was winter wind on his back.

Close, so close. Luke reached inside and invented a fresh burst of speed. He pulled away from the breath and towards the embrace of the desert night.

The hand, wide as his back from shoulder to shoulder, hit him then. The blow picked Luke up off his feet and pitched him through the air. He crashed, rolled, and finally looked over his shoulder at what hit him.

A shark stood in the desert.

The creature had the thick, muscular arms and legs of a man and the long, curved claws of… *something*, but everything else about it, from its blue-white skin to the dorsal fin on its back, was pure and utter shark.

Purest of all was its head. The keg-sized head with its black eyes and chainsaw teeth that were wholly and totally that of a Shark.

There was one other human thing about it, though. Rage. The gigantic shark was trembling with it.

"He killed our sister," it said. Somewhere, inside the blender of its intonation, he recognized a twinge of West's voice.

"…Jack?" Luke asked.

The Shark only stalked closer, quickly covering the ground it had thrown Luke across. Luke scrambled back on all fours, leaving a trail of wet dirt between his legs as his bladder let go.

A small stone lay in the path of West's hunter's tread. The Shark kicked it aside without even realizing it was there. The stone clattered away with a staccato sound neither of them paid any attention to.

But if they had, they might have heard the inorganic sound underneath it. A single, mechanical *clink*. In truth, it

was no more than the sound of a toenail
clipper at work.

West took another step and then a
pillar of earth and fire rose up behind it
with a rattling boom.

West roared and stumbled. Luke
screamed. A whizzing piece of shrapnel
nicked his cheek and drew blood.

Luke was back up before the last of
the dust settled. Running again, driven
by a terror more intense than anything
he'd ever felt in his comfortable,
privileged life. He ran blind, lost in
darkness and fear. And he welcomed it.
Dove into it. He hurtled through that
darkness and prayed nothing would
ever find him again.

Light found him. A brick wall of it
stopped him in his tracks.

"DON'T MOVE!" a voice boomed,
amplified by a speaker. *"GET DOWN
ON THE GROUND AND PUT YOUR
HANDS BEHIND YOUR HEAD!"*

"Who's there!?" Luke called. He
squinted, trying to see who, or what,
stood on the other side of the
smothering light. "I need your help,
please! I think- I think that she's hurt

but I don't know! We need to get out of here!"

A silhouette broke the light. It came towards him. The backlighting was too strong for Luke make out any features. The figure remained nothing but a dark outline, even when they were almost face-to-face. But that didn't matter. All that mattered was-

It's a person. A regular person. Yes. YES.

Then, Luke saw more lights as the shadow struck him in the face and knocked him on his back.

He was still on the ground when a small, metal circle pressed against his head. Fireworks still bursting in his eyes, Luke couldn't see what it was, but the sharp *snap* of pistol cocking told him everything he needed to know.

"You hold real still now," the same voice said. There was no loud speaker boom now, but every word came out with that same loud, authoritarian swagger. "You move and you'll wish the Jack in the Box had caught you. That would have been quick. Me? I'm known for my patience" He jabbed the oily, metal circle harder against Luke's temple. "We clear?"

"He's naked, Martin," a second voice said from beyond the light. This one was thin and reedy. It carried no authority and precious little intelligence. "Why's he naked?"

"Because he's a diversion," the gruff shadow, Martin, growled. Rough hands hauled Luke up and dragged him past the glare of the light. Luke had time to realize it was a spotlight mounted on the roll bar of a Jeep Wrangler before he was shoved face first onto the hood. His arm was twisted behind his back and wrenched upwards to the breaking point.

"Where's the rest of your unit?" Martin snarled.

"What unit!? What the fuck are you talking about!?"

Martin yanked him up by the hair and then slammed him back down hard enough to knock out a tooth.

"You've still got legs, so clearly you weren't the one who triggered the perimeter mine. That says there's at least two of you. And you ran right into our patrol, doing everything you could, including stripping bare-ass, to make sure you had our attention. That means you've got other operatives infiltrating our territory."

"You're not listening to me. There's something-"

"Mueller, get on the radio and inform HQ we have a perimeter breach and likely Federal Government Operatives inside of our borders. Inform them that this is not, repeat, NOT a drill and that we're bringing a prisoner in for interrogation."

Luke tried to lunge up and away, but he couldn't even budge an inch. This maniac, whatever else he was, was built out of solid muscle. True muscle. Luke's twice weekly personal training sessions couldn't compete.

"By the authority of the Nevada Nation of Patriots, you are under arrest for acts of espionage-"

"You fucking lunatics! *She's looking for me!*"

"Where your case will be assessed by a High Council review," Martin spoke over him. "As you are not a soldier of the NNP, no counsel will be afforded to you."

He lifted Luke up, with his arm still cranked between his shoulders, and marched him towards the back of the Jeep. Luke struggled about as successfully as a sack of flour. He ended up in a heap in the backseat, staring up from the floor at a skinny kid in military surplus fatigues manning the spotlight.

The kid was not looking back at Luke, though. He was staring out into desert with big, bulging eyes.

"CONTACT!" he screamed.

Martin's reaction was immediate. He trained his sidearm on the circle of rocks and dirt caught in the spotlight's glare. He waited two full breaths, but nothing moved.

"Coordinates!" he barked.

"Te-" Mueller stuttered. "I mean, eleven o'clock. I don't… Jesus I just saw it right at the edge of the light!" He panned the spotlight to the left. The light shook and jerked with the trembling of his hands.

"Keep it steady," Martin warned.

"I only saw it for a second! It's huge, Martin! Huge!"

The hand that descended from the shadows was indeed huge. It wrapped completely around Mueller's waist and lifted him up.

The kid screamed. Martin wheeled around just in time to see a shark, a fucking *shark,* stick Mueller's entire torso into the jagged-edged halo of its jaws. The kid kept screaming.

"Noo! Nooo!"

The Shark bit down. Mueller came apart like a slow-cooked piece of pork. The desert wind grabbed his blood and sprayed it over the Jeep. Gore spattered Luke like rain.

Martin squeezed off three shots. The target was too large to possibly miss; all three struck the creature's central mass.

West took the .45 caliber rounds like they were pebbles. The milita's perimeter mine had been a modified M-67 grenade. West had taken the full brunt of the shrapnel in its back and legs and it had done little more than slow the Shark down. The bullets to the chest didn't even make it flinch.

The Jeep was between them. West pushed the vehicle aside with careless ease and thundered towards Martin.

The militia captain fought back a scream. There were no thoughts of patriotism or honor in his head now. Only a running tally of his trigger finger as he pumped bullets into the bloody-mouthed thing bearing down on him.

4...5...6...7

One bullet left. Martin pressed the pistol to his own head without hesitation.

West's massive hand closed around Martin's before he could pull the trigger. There was a muffled *bang* as the shot went off in West's clenched fist, but it was drowned out by Martin's shrieks as West crumpled his hand. He opened his mouth and howled out into the night.

West opened its mouth as well.

The Shark's mouth was wider. It left nothing behind of Martin except for his feet. Entrails dangling from her jaws, West pivoted back towards the Jeep. Luke saw her coming and that was the last time he looked back. He clamored up into the driver's seat. The motor was still running. He shifted into drive and slammed on the gas.

The Jeep surged forward, peeling out in a haze of rock and dust. West lunged after it.

Any other time, and West could have grabbed the Jeep by the bumper, flipped it over, and pulled the whimpering, naked wretch free like clam meat from the shell. But the only semi-serious injury West had suffered from the booby trap was a shard of shrapnel embedded in the back of its knee. It slowed the Shark down just enough that the Jeep got up to speed just before it could get in range, and West's questing claws closed on empty air instead of the back of the Jeep. The Shark belly-flopped into the dirt and roared out its fury as the Jeep became nothing but taillights fading into the distance.

Already almost a mile away, Luke clearly heard her final call. He pressed down on the gas a little harder.

19

Jack hated interviews. Always had. It was just that there only so many times you could repeat the same answers to the same questions without getting impatient.

"No, not fans," he repeated. Again. "They didn't even know who I was."

The cop wasn't even taking notes anymore. He just nodded.

Jack was starting to hate this cop. This tall, stone-faced cop repeating the same shit over and over again in the same mechanical voice.

"And you have no idea which one of them put the cougar in your car?"

Funny that it should be the new question that put him over the edge. Jack stood up. He threw down his cup of cheap coffee and shoved off the blanket the cop had wrapped around his shoulders.

"One of them *was* the Cougar," Jack snarled. "One of them is still out there with my friend, and I have no idea what the fuck she is. Are you even looking for Luke? I gave you the fucking car, or do you need me to clarify that a thousand times too?"

Officer Iron Mask didn't even blink. "We're looking for the vehicle you described, the Porsche and the trucks." The cop's voice didn't waver, but something twitched at the corner of his eye.

"One of *my* friends is dead on the side of the road a few miles from here, so we are very diligently looking for the people you described. What we're not looking for is a bunch of *Twilight* rejects with magic animal powers. And for every minute you're here wasting my time with that bullshit, the more I start to wonder if the famous celebrity might have something he's keeping from us."

"You saw it in the store!" Jack screamed. "You think I made that thing up!?"

"I don't know what that fucking thing is," the cop hissed. "It's so burnt, nobody's going to know what it is for another week. I've got nothing concrete right now except for you, Rockstar." The cop stepped back. He straightened his hat and his expression straightened along with it.

"Why don't you think about that while I get you another cup of coffee. You seemed to have spilled yours."

The cop, California Highway Patrol Sergeant Miguel Gomez, went back into the ruins of the snack-mart. He made his way over broken glass and pools of blood to the coffee station and filled a cup for Galindo, but he didn't bring it back out right away. He poured a cup for himself and took a sip, not even wincing at the scalding heat. Inside of the store, the stench of the burnt… *thing* underneath the tarp was horrendous, but Gomez toughed it out.

Time. All the cop could do was kill as much of it as he could and hope that somewhere, out there on the roads, other officers were having better luck than he was.

As if summoned, the radio crackled next to his ear. Gomez involuntarily held his breath.

"Gomez?"

Miguel exhaled. Shit.

"He still there, Carson?"

"Right where you left him. I've got an update on the ambulance."

"And?"

"An hour away. At least. Six car pile up on the Interstate south of Bonnie Claire. Early word is three dead and two dozen injured. Nobody's gonna spare a full rig for a guy who's already bandaged and stable. Doesn't matter how many platinum albums he's got." Carson laughed. *"It's almost like being rich and famous doesn't get you special treatment in this country."*

Gomez knew Carson was just trying to keep him on the level, but he was in no mood to appreciate it. He desperately wanted that ambulance. "Jackie" Galindo was either lying, crazy, or coming down off a serious high, and Gomez wanted to get a blood sample while everything in his system was still fresh.

No reason to dawdle in the burnt stench anymore. Gomez grabbed Galindo's coffee and started back out to the curb.

"We've got another problem, partner."

Gomez didn't have to ask, he came out of the snack-mart and saw the problem for himself.

Six car pile up. Not enough EMTs to spare.

But plenty of reporters to go around. No matter how much blood got spilled, there always more than enough of those mosquitos with microphones to go around. They crowded at the police tape, some of them snapping pictures of the CSI tech cataloging evidence by the gas pump. Others framed their live shots so they got one of the rookies interviewing the surviving clerk in the background.

Those were the semi-respectable ones. The rest focused on one thing and one thing only, on the big, scary shock rocker sitting on a bench with his face all fucked up and his eyes staring at something a million miles away.

Gomez made the call. "Leave the rookies with the techs, put Hettinger in charge. Then bundle up our VIP. We'll take him to the Road Station until we can free up a medic to take a blood sample."

"What if he refuses?"

167

"Tell him that's the best place to wait for updates on his friend."

No need to coddle Galindo anymore. Gomez poured his coffee out on the curb and then went to collar the man himself and wait for Carson to bring the car around.

Wait for updates on his friend.

That was another question mark. Luke Barinski. It checked out that he was Galindo's agent, and he wasn't answering his phone. But that didn't mean that he was out there somewhere in the desert, at the mercy of a beautiful blonde in a Porsche Boxster. ("Do you know the license number, Mr. Galindo?" No, of course not.) And it definitely didn't prove the existence of some werecougar. Gomez had seen a lot of crazy shit in the desert, but most of it was crazy people. Not boogeymen.

Excuse me, Boogeywomen.

His radio crackled again. Gomez stopped, still out of Galindo's earshot.

"By the way, the plates on that Mustang came back. They match a Ford F-150 in West Virginia."

"So fakes, like we expected."

"A little more interesting than what we expected. The plates went missing eight years ago, about the same time the truck's owner was found deceased. Coroner's report says the guy had been mauled to death. Mountain Lion most likely.

Carson chuckled.

"I think this is just the break we were looking for, partner."

"Bring the car around and stay off the damn open channel," was all Gomez had to say.

20

Luke didn't have his phone. He didn't have Google Maps or a GPS.

He didn't have any fucking clothes.

What he did have was a map he had no clue how to read and no idea where the hell he was going.

That hadn't mattered at first. For a long time, the only things Luke cared about were speed and distance. It took twenty minutes of driving for Luke to realize that he was looking around and there was not a single manmade *anything* to be seen around him. No lights, no roads, definitely no buildings. It was like he was driving around on the surface of Mars.

If he were on his own, that would have been fine. He could drive through the middle of nowhere until the sun came up and been perfectly happy so long as he didn't run into any paramilitary groups or… anything with fins.

Except he wasn't on his own.

He killed our sister.

That was what West had said, and the pure hatred in her voice had been even more chilling than the monstrous thing she'd become.

Luke hadn't been the one she really wanted.

That means I have to find Jack before she does.

Or before her brothers did.

Another fifteen minutes of driving brought him to a road.

Maybe.

It wasn't paved. It was more dirt and rock, like every other God forsaken thing around him, but at least it was packed down. It resembled something manmade. Luke looked left and right and saw nothing civilized at either end of the horizon. He tried to visualize where he was in relation to the highway and came up empty. No surprise there, he couldn't get from Venice to Hollywood without Google Maps.

Fuck it, he turned left.

Luke followed the "road." He kept his headlights off. Navigating the path was harder by moonlight, but he couldn't forget that *she* was still out there.

Luke kept waiting for his fear to stop feeling so… *immediate*, but it never did. Not even now, in the relative safety of the moving vehicle. The only time he'd ever felt anything like this was that time in college when Cass told him she was late. It was the same constant, pressing dread that he felt now. Same knots in his stomach. Same crushing clamps at his eyes.

And no way to fix it. Nothing to do but keep feeling this way until something changes.

But nothing changed in the darkness. Not even the scenery. The same shadows and emptiness rattled past him over and over again. He tried to stay focused on the road, but the monotony around him was no match for the vivid life of his memories.

West above him. Perfect, firm, high breasts. Delectably tapered waist. Long, slender neck.

Eyes black as tar. Mouth crowded with broken glass teeth.

A gun, a motherfucking gun, pressed against his head.

The shark again, huge and terrible, lunging for the Jeep.

If I'd gotten into the driver's seat even a second later…

A shadow ran up at the edge of his vision, something big and only getting bigger. Luke slammed on the brakes. No seatbelt, his sternum compressed against the steering wheel and left him choking for air, but not so injured he couldn't struggle for reverse. The Jeep hurtled backwards, pulling Luke back away from-

He hit the brakes again. His head slammed into the headrest.

It was a horse. Tail swishing as it trotted along the edge of a ranch fence, craning its head closer for a sniff at the passing vehicle.

And, further back, there was a small ranch house with a blue light flickering in the living room window.

TV light.

People. Awake people.

The road he was on curved. Luke followed it right up into the driveway of the ranch house and turned off the engine. He got out of the car and, at the touch of his feet on the gravel, remembered that he was naked.

Christ, how the fuck am I going to knock on someone's door at 3 o'clock in the morning and ask to use their phone like this?

Maybe trying to hold onto his composure was a mistake. Maybe he would be better off flinging himself at the door, screaming and crying and begging for help. That feeling was there already, maybe there was no sense in trying to keep it in check.

The debate was settled for him by a sharp, ominous *CHIK-CHAK* from the shadows beside the garage. It was a universal sound, but one that Luke only knew from video games and movies. The sound of a pump-action shotgun loading a round.

"Don't move, pervert," an aged, hardened voice called out from the shadows.

The decision was out of his hands, though. Luke's knees crumpled of their own accord. He moaned and cupped his hands pitifully over his genitals.

"Please," he moaned. "Please don't shoot me. I'm not here to hurt you, I swear… I need help, okay? That's it. Please." He wanted to explain. He wanted to be persuasive and smooth and convincing, but the words wouldn't come out. To speak them was to relive them.

And I won't. I can't. I can't see it again.

Luke wept beneath a stranger's gunsights. He cried and shuddered and hugged himself, hurt and afraid and so damn exhausted.

I want to be home. I want to be at a party. I want some tequila and I want a nice suit and I want some blow. I want my mother. I want to go to bed. I want this to stop.

Warm hands cupped his face. Dry, rough hands, permanently baked by years in the sun, but they cradled him with such gentleness. They pulled him up and gently set his head on a shoulder clad in terry cloth that smelled like herbs.

"It's alright," that sun-smoked voice whispered. "You're alright. I've got you, brother."

Luke drifted off for what happened next. It felt *okay* to drift off. More, it felt *necessary.* He vaguely realized that he was led inside while that scorched voice murmured off-key lyrics in his ear. "Bringing in the Sheep," and "Like a Bridge Over Troubled Water." The words washed over him with the warmth of a summer tide.

She sat him on a scratchy, sunken couch that was the most comfortable thing he'd ever been on. There was blissful silence and then she was back with crisp white bandages and soothing creams. She wrapped his wound and pulled cactus needles and splinters from his skin. Then, words again in his ear.

"Now you just wait right here while I get you some clothes."

Ok. Fine. Great. Luke lay down on the couch. *The best couch ever.* Really and truly. This was what the womb was like. This was perfect protection and peace.

"At this point, the involvement of shock rocker Jackie Galindo has been confirmed, though in what capacity, we cannot yet say."

He didn't want to look. Nope. Didn't even want to open his eyes. Just fine like this, thanks for asking.

But look he did.

The woman's TV was still on, tuned to one of the 24 hour news channels. The middle-aged, botox-ed newswomen stood with a Mobil station framed behind her. Police tape ran from one edge of it to the other.

And he saw a familiar Mustang crumpled against a wall in the background.

"...We have reports of at least one fatality, but at this time there's no official statement as to what happened here or what exactly Jackie Galindo was doing at the scene."

They cut to a long shot of Jack then. Sitting on the curb, wrapped in a blanket. The screen split then. Jack, wrapped in a blanket on one side; on the other side, a file photo of Jackie Galindo decked out in makeup, real teeth and painted teeth pulled back in matching snarls while jets of fire flared up behind him.

The woman came back with a folded bundle of clothes.

"One of my boys left these. You're a little on the skinnier side, but they'll do alright."

For the first time, Luke actually saw his caretaker. She was a thin women with a lined face and close cut hair the color of sand. She reminded him of one of the desert trees, long and gnarled and indisputably immortal. She wore a pale green robe and a simple wooden cross hung at the open expanse of her neck. She had a folded shirt and a pair of pants held out in his direction.

"At this point, there's been no response from Galindo or his representatives."

She followed his gaze to the TV.

"Looks like you weren't the only one who had a patch of trouble tonight."

"Where is that?" Luke asked.

"Not far actually," the woman said. "Maybe twenty minutes east once you're back on the highway." She extended the bundle of clothes a little more in his direction. Luke took the clothes without looking away from the TV screen. There was a closeup now; Jackie getting bundled into a squad car.

There. Problem solved. Jack's with the cops now, you've got nothing to worry about.

Luke turned his focus to the clothes. The shirt had buttons. Very tricky, buttons. Had to line them up just right. It was a flannel shirt, and the jeans were so faded by the wash they were almost white. He stood up and pulled on the jeans.

Static crackled. Not from the TV.

"Home base, this is Carson and Gomez, 10-19 back to base. We've got a... "VIP" with us, please make sure we've got a room ready for him."

"Easy," the woman soothed. "That's just my police scanner. Or it was my late husband's anyway. He had it because he was a deputy. I kept it because sometimes I can't sleep and I like to listen to it and the news and get a piece of the rest of the world. It's nothing for you to worry about."

You said it, lady. I've got nothing to worry about. I'm all good.

As if to prove his point, the TV zoomed in on Jack getting gently sheparded into the back of a cop car.

There you go. Jack's taken care of. He's on his way to a whole building full of cops. Nothing- I mean, no one, is going to be able to touch him there.

"Do you need to talk to the police?" The woman pressed. "Is that what you're trying to tell me?"

He's fine now. And you've done enough. Shit, you've SURVIVED enough. Whatever gesture you wanted to make for Jack, you've made it. Ask this woman to help you get home. If you want to do something else for Jack, get on the phone and get his lawyer up here. "Make some calls," how good does that sound right about now?

"…Maybe you should lay back down," she said. "There's soup I can heat up."

There's no maybe about it, Luke thought.

But what he said was, "Can you tell me how to get to the police station? …And do you have a pair of boots I could borrow?"

21

Jack slumped down in the hard-backed chair. It was far from comfortable, but he'd slept in worse places than this. He'd slept in the back of cars, in the storage room of run-down clubs, and crammed in the back of a box truck with a drummer, an overweight bass player, two roadies, and one tour manager.

And he'd never been this exhausted in his life. Not after they played three full sets at Riot fest, and not after spending 36 hours locked in the studio with Rob Zombie. He could've passed out against a cactus and slept until the damn thing grew another two feet.

But if his need to sleep was an irresistible force, his anxiety over Luke was an immovable object. He didn't want to even close his eyes until he knew *something* about what happened to him. The resulting stalemate left Jack in a no man's land of physical, mental, and spiritual exhaustion.

Could be worse, a sour voice reminded him. *You could be Luke. Wonder what he's doing right now- maybe West is offering the same special East offered you. A leg in a trashcan here, an arm out the window a few miles further down the road. Hey, Jackie, there's a song title for you- "Entrail Treasure Trail."*

Aw, Christ! He tried to push back from the table and only succeeded in pressing his throbbing back harder against the unmoving metal.

Of course. Because the chair's bolted to the floor. Because I'm in a goddamn interrogation room.

"For his own security," they had said. Bullshit. They thought he was either crazy or in on something, so they had him in a room one step up from a holding cell- a cinderblock room with nothing inside except for a bolted-down table and chair, and nobody for company except his own reflection in the two-way mirror.

He swigged cheap coffee and ran his hands through the stubble of his shaved head.

If I had a nice lawyer's haircut, maybe then they'd let me be a victim. I would have gotten a couch if I was a nice white boy in a suit.

He dropped back in the chair and let his head fall against the tabletop. The cheap metal reeked of cigarettes and sweat.

...Luke would have gotten me a couch.

-   -   -

Officer Peter Flegar went back to the front desk and his Netflix. The stream was paused right where he left it. His bag of Fritos was right where he left it.

His coffee, just the right temperature when Flegar had left it, was now lukewarm sludge.

Thank you very fucking much, Sergeant Gomez. Flegar went back to the break room for another cup, still stewing about the way Gomez had thrown a set of keys at him like a fucking valet.

"Car 54 is due for an oil change. Take it around to the garage."

Yes, sir, Flegar steamed. *Right away, Massa. But if it's alright, I left your shotgun in the cab instead of checking it back into the armory. I just hope I'm on shift to see your fucking face when the violation turns up in your inbox.*

Finally settled down again, Officer Flegar fished out another handful of Fritos and stuffed them into his mouth. The crunch of fracturing chips echoed in the lobby of the road station, uncontested by the usual chatter from the breakroom or guys working on reports at their desks. Between the pileup on the 15 and the manhunt for whatever freak had ripped open 'ol Ben Grillo, every Highway Patrolman on duty was out in the field. The station was completely empty except for himself, the cute redhead working dispatch, and now Carson, Gomez (Asshole), and their little pussy boy.

Flegar snorted, remembering the sight of Jackie "The Devil of Dia De Los Muertos" Galindo dragging his feet across the lobby with Gomez right alongside him like a crossing guard escorting a retard across the street.

184

Pussies. All of those guys- get them off stage, get them out from behind their bodyguards, and you'd be lucky to find enough spine to make a single backbone between the lot of them.

There was a lesson there for when he had kids someday. Anyone can look like a badass in a ten million dollar music video. Real tough guys went out and did it for real every day.

Of course, he thought, *I should probably get married before I have a kid.* That got him thinking about dispatch girls again. Sure, redheaded Milla was cute, but the blonde that came in for the morning shift? Kala? Jesus Christ, that woman had a body built for Pornhub.

From that point on, the actual raising of children seemed more like an inadvertent side effect than anything else.

The swinging double doors jerked him loose from visions of handcuffs and blondes who'd do anything to get out of a ticket. Flegar sat up, brushed crumbs from his shirt, and tried to look attentive.

A man came in. A man so tall, he had to duck down to get through the door.

"What can I do for you, sir?" Flegar asked.

The big man ignored him. He stood in the entryway and snorted. The sound was so low, primal, and sudden, Flegar couldn't help but jump in his seat.

"Sir?"

Snort. Snort. The guy went to the case where the citations and awards were displayed, and took another big sniff at the air. His barrel chest swelled and almost burst.

Just what I need- some freakshow tripping out of his goddamn mind. And, of course, he's got to be the size of Brock Lesnar.

Flegar thought of radioing Carson for support, but decided against it. Carson had a streak of pussy himself, and if he got involved there'd be paperwork and processing and all that crap nobody wanted to do at three o'clock in the morning. And Flegar wasn't looking to arrest the big idiot. He just wanted to… move him along a little.

Flegar slipped his baton from its holster. Just what the doctor ordered- no taser cartridges or pepper spray canisters to be accounted for, just the firm assurance of the rubber-grip handle in his hand. He drew closer to the big weirdo.

"Alright, pal. How about we turn it around?"

The guy didn't turn around. His head was still up. His nostrils flared, trying to catch some odor Flegar was not privy to.

"Come on, guy. Lots of good stuff to smell outside. What do you say?"

Reluctantly, Flegar grabbed the guy's arm. It was not a pleasant experience. Up close, the guy's clothes were positively rank, and there was something dry and rancid crusted up in his beard.

Flegar pulled, but the guy would not be moved. He gave no indication that he even noticed Flegar was touching him.

"He's here," the big guy murmured. Flegar didn't know what that meant, and he didn't care. *"Ask Nice Twice."* That was Flegar's approach to police work. Ask Nice Twice. After that, Ask Hard And Only Ask Once.

Flegar swung his police baton. He leveraged all of his considerable mass behind a high, arcing shot that struck the freakshow along the top curve of his skull. It was a good spot to hit; hurt like hell, but the skull was strong there and unlikely to crack. Flegar connected with a satisfying *CRUNCH* that he felt all the way up to his shoulder. He stepped back and waited for the big guy to drop.

The big guy did not drop. The big guy had apparently not gotten the message that he'd been hit with a shot that would have put a protester on his back for a month. He stayed right where he was. Didn't even sway.

It was Flegar's baton that had *CRUNCHED*. The truncheon in his hand was now bent at a 45 degree angle.

Still not looking at Flegar, the giant's hand pistoned out. He broke off three of Flegar's teeth as he forced his fingers into the cop's mouth. Flegar let out a muffled moan, and then the fingers in his mouth began to swell and lengthen. Flegar felt *hairs* sprout and prickle against his tongue.

North clenched his changing hand just as the claws began to form. He sliced the cop's tongue to ribbons and ripped his jaw off all in the same savage stroke.

Flegar's eyes bulged. The bottom of his face had become a gore sprinkler. Blood gushed out where screams no longer could. He hosed the reception seating and glass display case in a spray of red.

Flegar collapsed. His blood pooled around North's boots. Boots that were already splitting apart as the feet inside of them cracked, shifted, and grew. Black claw tips pierced through the steel toes.

The doors swung open again behind him. A familiar scent joined the room.

"Do we wait?" South asked. What he meant was, *"Do we wait for West?" "Do we wait and get our revenge as a family?"*

A low growl rumbled out from a mouth that no longer sat flat on North's face. His lips bulged out, accompanied by a sound like popping packing bubbles as bones broke and reformed beneath the skin.

Answer enough. South's own tan flesh had become dry and cracked, morphing into a necrotic shade of gray. His eyes became brighter, as if his irises were flooding with something luminous and toxic green.

No waiting then. The sister-killer paid now.

22

Marcia hadn't been able to go back to sleep.

She prided herself on her kindness and her devotion to the ideal of Christian charity. So when that scared, confused (naked) man showed up on her doorway, there was no question that she would do whatever she could to help him. The desert was a strange place, full of strange people, and this was not the first time she'd played the Samaritan to someone lost and wandering in the dark. And Marcia had served tonight as faithfully as she always did. She bandaged his wounds and clothed his nakedness. She offered him shelter and when he declined, she gave him directions to where he wanted to go. As soon as his taillights disappeared into the night, she should have been in bed sleeping the sleep of the just.

So what was she doing still up in her easy chair?

And why couldn't she shake the feeling that she hadn't done a damn thing to help that poor boy?

Answers eluded her, even when she sought solace in prayer. The nagging certainty she'd done wrong kept her awake and watching the news, even after reports of… whatever had happened at the Mobil station gave way to updates on the latest violence in the Holy Lands.

The Police. Maybe that's where I failed. I should have convinced him to wait for them to come to him instead of the other way around. At least then I'd know for sure he got where he wanted to go.

Instead, the last thing she knew for certain about her "guest" was that she'd found him weeping and naked and she'd let him walk right back out the door. Clothed, true, but still with a look of such dread on his face. She had a brother who died in the Tet Offensive, and he had the same look in his eyes the last time she saw him alive.

Remembering her brother was the final straw. The need for a drink had been gnawing at her ever since her visitor drove off, and she was tired of fending it off. She went into the kitchen for a glass and for the bottle of Makers that had been sitting in the freezer ever since her husband died.

The knock came at her door. Slow and light, like a shy trick or treater. The sound was ice water in her ear, dripping steadily deeper with every knock. She waited. Afraid to move. Hoping it was only the wind.

It came again.

Knock.

Knock.

Silent as she could, careful to avoid the windows, Marcia crept back into the living room.

Knock.

Knock.

Her door was always open. Always. Illegal immigrants, teenage runaways, anyone at anytime. It was on a plaque next to her door. Revelations 3:20.

"Open the door, I will come in, and we will share a meal together as friends."

Marcia didn't want this friend. She felt the certainty of it deep in her chest.

That was no friend on the other side of the door.

I'll just wait. I won't make a sound and whoever's out there will just move on and leave me in peace.

Or maybe she should get the shotgun back out from the closet. Two floorboards creaked, but she knew which ones and knew how to avoid them.

The door swung open. Except for the groan as the frame broke, it swung inwards with barely a whisper.

The woman stood in Marcia's doorway. Like the man, she too was naked. Unlike the man, she was not weeping. And she was not afraid.

Marcia's breath caught in her throat. Not at the stranger's beauty, which was undeniable, but because there was something… *unholy* about this woman. She stood in the doorway, disconnected and silent, but she reminded Marcia of an unplugged tablesaw. Motionless for the moment, but only a flipped switch away from coming to deadly life.

The woman took a step inside. Marcia took a matching step backwards.

The woman, a blonde, stood in the foyer with her chin slightly raised. Her nostrils flared.

"There was a man here," West said. "He was bleeding." Another step forward. Marcia took another step backwards.

"His smell stops here… Is that because he's here?"

West's blank, cold eyes, flicked downwards. She took another step forward and this time Marcia had no step backwards to take. Her back pressed against the unyielding kitchen wall.

But it was not her that West wanted. The blonde nudged the first aid kit off of the coffee table. Aspirin and disinfectant clattered out. A roll of gauze tumbled out and came to a stop between Marcia's feet.

"You stopped his bleeding. That's why I don't have his scent anymore."

Marcia didn't answer. Her eyes were fixed directly ahead. Not at West's face, but directly over the blonde's shoulder. Marcia kept a mirror on the wall there, and it offered her an unobstructed view of the woman's bare back.

The reflected flesh was a ruin. It was a patchwork of deep gouges, crusty with dried blood. Bits of blackened metal dotted her back like grotesque seasoning.

"I need to know where he went," West said.

Marcia looked away from the woman's reflection and into her eyes. She tried to speak but all that came out was a dry croak. She'd found rattlesnakes in her barn before. She thought that nothing else on Earth could have eyes as cold and wicked as those snakes did.

She was wrong.

West stalked closer. "Do you hear what I'm saying to you?" She spoke slowly and clearly and chose her Meat Words with great care. It was not easy. She longed to speak in her True Voice, but the True Language only had words of hatred, hunger, and family. It was not a language of questions.

"I need to know where he went," West repeated. "When you tell me, you get to die."

It was the last thing West said in her Meat Voice before casting aside her Meat Face.

If Marcia hadn't been listening, then she was in for a very long night.

23

"Here."

Gomez's gaze never wavered, but he took the coke Carson offered and drained half of it in a single draught.

"Has he played *Settling The Reaper's Tab* yet? That one's my favorite."

As usual, he failed to make his partner crack a smile. Galindo had finally passed out. He was laying there, face down on the table, and Gomez just kept staring at him through the one-way mirror, like Galindo was just waiting for him to blink so that he could make a break for it.

"…Wait a minute," Carson said. He looked from his partner, to the musician, and then back again. "Are you actually waiting for him to try and make a break for it?"

"I don't like him," Gomez said. "I don't like his story. I don't like his mystery friend that nobody is able to find, and I don't like that torched…whatever the hell it was that we found in the gas station."

"Well, since we're getting things off our chest, does it bother you that he's sticking to his 'Cougar woman abducted me!' narrative? Because I'll be honest, that's what I don't like. Yeah, it sounds like it's crazy or bullshit, but he's not acting like a bullshitter and he's not acting like he's crazy."

Gomez never got a chance to answer. Something struck him from behind and lifted him up and off his feet; hit him and manhandled him in a way he hadn't experienced since he was an eight-year-old squirt.

That was the thought, eerily calm, that raced with him as he soared weightlessly across the room.

I am in the third grade again. Robbie Forrester has just shoved me from behind. I'm going to hit my chin on the curb and need four stitches.

He did not hit the curb. He hit the one-way mirror and kept going right through it. Jagged edges of glass and thin metal ripped the skin from his face and punctured his jugular. Shards beset him from all sides and grated his flesh like shredded cheese.

The man standing in the observation room had been large, strong, and competent. The thing that came out the other side of the looking glass was more raw meat than man.

- - -

Jack dreamt the room was filled with a surreal rain of glass and blood. He lifted his head up just a second before a gore-drenched sack of raw meat and rags splattered across the table. He should have been revolted but, safe in the dreamscape, he was stunned by the grotesque beauty of it. Time had seemed to slow down. Slow enough that he could see the thing skid across the tabletop and appreciate the graceful flapping of the bloody strips of khaki streaming behind it.

A limp, red log of tenderloin, certainly not a *human leg,* slapped a bloody streak across his face and knocked him out of his chair.

The fall hurt. He scrambled on all fours and shook his head. Awake or asleep? He'd bitten his tongue. The hot, iron taste in his mouth told him he was awake.

The gigantic Bear framed in the shattered mirror told him there was no way that could be true.

It was the avatar of all bears-covered in thick, knotted brown fur, so tall it had to crouch to fit underneath an eight-foot-tall ceiling. Its features were too large to be natural. Its eyes were shot glasses brimming with hatred and fury too articulate to belong to a mere animal.

The Bear bellowed. The low, rumbling sound shook the glass on the floor.

Beneath the bass roar, Jack heard the echo of a voice.

East's brother.

"Jesus fucking Christ!"

That was the other cop, the one who wasn't such an asshole. He drew his gun and aimed up, way up, right at the side of the freak Bear's head.

A green blur streaked past the cop before he could fire. After it passed, the cop wasn't just missing his gun. He was missing both of his hands.

The cop shrieked. Blood gushed from the ragged stumps of his wrists.

The Alligator rose back up from beneath the bottom edge of the mirror. Blood caked its snout. Its green eyes shone with dark glee. It rose up on its hind legs, not as tall as the Bear but heavy with solid muscle.

Jack had a brief flash. Two brothers, one towering and shaggy, the other squat and powerful.

The Alligator fell upon the screaming cop. It drove Carson down to the ground and bit into the soft meat beneath his ribs.

North came towards Jack. The Bear bellowed and pushed apart the remnants of the wall, forcing its way into the interrogation room.

Nightmare or waking, Jack's scramble for the door was the same. He twisted the doorknob and flung himself against the door in the same rushing motion.

The handle didn't even jiggle. He bounced harmlessly off the locked door.

Jack took the only protection there was left. He scrambled under the table, certain that it didn't matter. He was-

-   -   -

Going to die.

The table was bolted to the floor, but North tossed it aside with absurd ease.

And there was the sister-killer.

That was North's last thought that could be considered an actual thought: *This tiny, cowering thing somehow murdered East.* After that, animal rage cast its Meat Mind aside. The Bear grabbed Jack by the neck and lifted him up. It brought the weak, tiny Meatkind right up to bite off his weak, tiny Meat Face. Jack flung his hands up, pitifully trying to protect himself.

If North had held onto a little more of its Meat Mind, it might have noticed that the weak, tiny human's hands were not empty.

-   -   -

Jack flung the handful of broken mirror shards right into the Bear's face. Most of the shards bounced harmlessly off the creature's thick hide, but a single jagged sliver of glass found purchase. The shard hit the Bear's eye and slit the dark orb wide open.

North howled. Pain this time, not fury. The brown fur around its eye turned gushing red.

Jack twisted and fell from the Bear's grasp. The door behind him was still locked. No other choice, he scrambled low past the bear and kept running. He didn't even notice the breath of air pass over the top of his head, a breath that was the bottom edge of a paw swinging past him with the force of a falling tree.

He leapt over the bottom of the mirror frame and into the observation room. He landed in a slick of Carson's blood and nearly fell flat on his face, but kept running.

South lifted its snout up from the hollowed remains of the cop's chest and lunged for Jack. Its teeth closed on the empty air where Jack's leg had been only a second earlier. The Alligator's jaws didn't close with a *snap;* they closed with a thunderclap.

All Jack cared about was the door. If this one was locked too, his next step was the last one he'd ever take.

The door handle turned beneath his hand and Jack was in the hallway.

"HELP!" he screamed. "JESUS CHRIST, SOMEBODY!"

South spared one glance for its brother. North had fallen to one knee, but the Bear had stopped groaning. Blood still poured down its ruined eye, but the hatred in its other eye was rapidly focusing.

Its brother would be alright. The Alligator hissed and dropped to all fours.

It ran faster that way.

24

Jack ran without any idea where he was going. He careened through the hallways of the patrol station, bouncing off ugly beige walls, knocking pictures to the floor. He moved with the blind simplicity of what he was- prey running from the predator.

And the predator was coming. The scrabble of its claws over linoleum, that maniacal skittering clatter, drowned out everything else around him.

And the sound was growing closer. Closer.

And there was a scent now- a stench of rotting meat breath growing stronger and stronger.

"Jack!? JACK!? Are you here!?"

A door at the end of the hallway burst open. Luke came through with an AK-47 cradled in his arms.

"Jack!" he cried.

And then, immediately after, "Oh shit, Jack, GET DOWN!"

Luke raised the rifle. Jack dove to the ground and covered his ears.

Luke didn't aim, he just squeezed the trigger and kept it squeezed. Recoil drove the gun wild, bullets plastered the ceiling and both walls. The air filled with debris and choking dust.

But in such a narrow corridor, accuracy was unavoidable. Luke lit the Alligator up. South roared as hollow point bullets hit it in a swarm.

Jack lay flat at the creatures' feet, eyes shut tight, thunder roaring in his ears. Grit clogged his nostrils. Something hot and wet spattered repeatedly across his neck and back. It went on and on until-

Clickclickclickclick.

Silence. Jack opened his eyes.

Luke still stood by the far door; smoke rose from the barrel of the assault rifle hanging at his side. The hallway between them looked like it had been run through a wood chipper.

Jack took his hands away from his ears. They came away red and glistening.

Blood. His hands and back were slick with it. He rolled over.

The Alligator slumped against the wall, wheezing irregularly. The bullet wounds in its carcass weren't holes, they were ragged gouges, as if its hide was stone and Luke had gone at it with a hammer and chisel. Blood flowed down it in rivers through its dry, craggy skin.

Cautiously, Jack scuttled away from it and stood up. He edged his way back towards Luke's side.

South didn't stir. Breath rattled out of its ruptured gizzard. Its eyes, dull and dim, hung downwards. The Alligator slouched further down, letting the wall take the entirety of its weight.

…Its eyes closed.

Almost as one, Luke and Jack exhaled.

South's eyes snapped open, full of venomous hatred and vivid green life. The Alligator roared and surged at them with blood pouring from its open maw.

Jack pushed Luke back through the door but there was no need, Luke was already running.

-    -   -

North heard its brother roar and picked up the pace. The Bear was already coming. It had risen up the moment it heard the gunshots. That it was now blind in one eye meant nothing. It heard its brother's bellow. It smelled South's blood and it smelled both humans, the sister-killer and West's Meatkind from the bar.

It didn't smell its sister, and some vestigial part of its Meat brain asked why that might be, but the Bear refused to listen to that kind of petty Meat anxiety. The only thing that mattered was that North and South could hunt and that the humans were there.

Soon, they would be everywhere.

25

The Gator ripped the door off its hinges and stampeded through the break room. It flung the small table across the room and nearly tore through the next door at the far end of the room.

…Nearly.

South stopped.

The bloodlust still boiled in its cold blood, and the pain ravaging its bullet-ridden body just made its eagerness all the more overwhelming. Bloodlust compelled South to push forward relentlessly, to run the sister-killer and his companion down to the ground and rip them to shreds

A small, mostly inarticulate, shred of cunning compelled it to wait.

South's hearing was exceptional. If the Meatkind were just on the other side of the door, panting and stamping as they ran for their lives, South would have heard them.

Right now, it heard nothing.

The Alligator swung around. It was in the break room, the portal between the front entrance and the inner workings of the patrol station. Here on one side was a couch and a flat screen TV. On the other side, a full kitchen and the small, glass partitioned room that was the dispatch station.

Dispatch had been North and South's first stop after the lobby. They'd ripped the petite redhead out from the glass booth and ripped her into pieces that were petite-er and redder still. Then, to make absolutely sure there were no interruptions, they'd smashed the dispatch console.

That door was open. South could see there was nobody hiding in there.

…But there were closets.

…Closets with the doors closed.

North finally thundered in. The Bear's shoulders caught the door frame and ripped it right out of the wall. South didn't flinch, even as shards of sheetrock pelted its ridged back.

North did not question its brother's injuries nor its stillness. North knew this posture well. South stood straight and absolutely still, as perfectly alert as his little cousins in the swamp.

The Alligator waited for the sign, for the small, inevitable flicker that would tell it where the Meatkinds were hiding.

- - -

Huddled in the pantry, Jack and Luke waited to hear the Alligator and the Bear thunder past. They waited.
Waited.
...*We're going to die*, Jack realized. And it was all because he just had to try and be clever. He had to pull Luke aside instead of just bolting when they had the chance. Maybe the Alligator would have run them down and chewed their legs off, but there was no maybe about it now. They were going to die in this pantry.

- - -

South remained perfectly static. It could stay like this for hours, patiently waiting for its pray to reveal it self.
North could not wait. The bear huffed impatiently. South flicked its poisonous green eyes at its brother. The
212

Gator hissed a warning, but the Bear would not be warned off. North rumbled closer and snarled. It made the dishes rattle in the cabinet.

Still hissing, South reluctantly slithered aside.

North stepped forward and kept stepping forward. The Bear did not wait.

The Bear hunted.

-    -   -

They heard North snarl. Wood crunched. Pressed against the back wall of the pantry, Luke and Jack clung to each other like children.

-    -   -

North ripped the closet door off its hinges.

Inside, it found only boxes of road flares, stacked traffic cones, and batteries.

No Meatkind.

No sister-killers.

Two closets left.

No, not two. One of the doors had Meat words on it. "Mechanic's Shop" The Alligator couldn't read them consciously, but it intuited the meaning. If the Meatkind had gone that way, South would have heard them fleeing.

That left just one hiding place left. The door with the Meat markings for "Pantry."

That was when the screaming began.

-   -   -

The scream went off right in Jack's ear. He thought for certain it was Luke, or maybe even himself. That it was a high, feminine shriek meant nothing. The sense of terror building in that pressure cooker of a pantry made gender meaningless. It could have easily been either one of them.

It wasn't.

-   -   -

The blonde dispatcher that Desk Patrolman Flegar so unflatteringly revered, Kala, was all too aware of

"Phlegm's" leering interest; but as far as creeps went, he wasn't the worst. He kept his comments to himself, and she never caught him with his phone surreptitiously pointed in her direction. For the most part, he was easy to ignore.

She couldn't ignore him now. Flegar was spread out across the lobby in a red smear, his mouth hung open even wider than the time she'd spilled water all over her white blouse.

Kala kept screaming. The ruins of Officer Flegar demanded that she scream and Kala obliged. She shrieked and shrieked, and when the wall ripped open and the two creatures came pouring through, she tried to scream louder, but she found that it just couldn't be done.

She was still trying when they swept over her. South twisted its hips and swung a tail as thick around as a telephone pole. The heavy appendage snapped her head back and Kala screamed no more. It shattered her neck and caved in her face. What was once Kala fell to the ground in complete silence.

Silence so complete, both Bear and Alligator easily heard the scrambling feet from inside the break room.

<u>26</u>

Jack and Luke bolted the moment they heard the rumbling of North and South going after the poor screaming soul in the lobby. They made it into the mechanic's garage just as that same scream was cut hideously short.

"Oh, fuck," Luke murmured. "Oh, fuck."

They're coming, Jack realized. And that was it. Not even a thought for the *who* behind the scream. That kind of thinking was a luxury that the hunted couldn't afford.

Inside the spacious garage were three cop cars. A crusier up on a lift, an SUV with the hood open and the engine missing, and one more in the middle. The police cruiser that Jack had arrived in.

"That one!" Jack screamed. He ran for it with Luke at his side, knowing that if the doors were locked, they were dead.

If the keys weren't in it, they were dead.

If North and South caught them first, they were dead.

At the cop car, the doors at least opened. Jack threw himself into the driver's seat. Luke flopped over the hood and scrambled for the passenger door.

There was a shotgun stowed vertically between the two seats. Jack saw it and dismissed it in the same instant. The gun was secured in place by a locked collar around the barrel.

He groped at the ignition switch and felt nothing. He checked the cup holder. He practically ripped down the visor.

No keys. Nothing. Icy fingers clawed at his throat.

"On the floor!" Luke screamed.

And there they were, right between Jack's feet. He scooped up the keys and jammed the car key into the ignition. He cranked it hard enough that the key snapped off in the slot. It didn't matter. The engine caught and rumbled to life.

The car had its trunk pointed towards the roll-up garage door, but there was no time to turn around. Jack shifted into reverse.

South scrambled into the garage on all fours, followed closely by North. The Bear, almost white with sheetrock dust, roared. Its bellow drowned out the engine, even as Jack slammed on the gas and rocketed backwards towards the roll-up door. The door was closed, but there was nothing else for it. They'd have to be fast enough to rip right through it.

North was faster. The Bear slammed its claws into the hood, almost the same way East had stopped the Mustang cold in its track, but the Bear's strength was something else entirely. North bellowed and flipped the car over like it was a shopping cart. Glass broke. The chassis twisted. The cruiser went flying end over end in a cacophony of flying glass and warping metal.

Inside, Jack and Luke were not buckled in. They flopped helplessly about the cabin of the cop car. Their heads cracked together, adding a toneless ringing to the rest of the chaos assaulting their ears. Luke blacked out immediately. Jack tumbled back against the window. Something hard and angular struck him in the mouth. He groped for it blindly.

The cruiser flipped again and then slammed into the SUV. It teetered briefly, balanced precariously on the passenger side, and then fell topside-down with a final *crunch.*

Still on all fours, the Alligator arrowed after the cop car the moment it stopped rolling. It flew in like a low-flying missile, letting loose a croaking roar as it dove through the broken driver's side window. It was going to hook the sister-killer out and leave him on the floor, half-disemboweled, for its brother to finish.

Then South could have the shooter all to itself.

The Alligator shot through the broken window and opened its jaws wide. It came in so fast, it didn't even realize there was a shotgun in its mouth until it had swallowed half of the barrel.

Jack spat blood and pushed on the shotgun, the ridge of the gunsight prodded the soft meat at the back of the Alligator's gullet. The bulky collar, and the bolts that had secured the shotgun before North had flipped the car, pressed at its throat.

South looked into Jack's sweat-ringed eyes. The Alligator saw terror there, terror and frantic desperation.

And it saw something else reflected there, something familiar, in the last moments before Jackie Galindo pulled the trigger.

The shotgun roared. South spasmed. Buckshot liquefied its innards.

Pain flared at the back of North's skull, the same grinding, shredding agony as when East died.

It didn't hurt nearly as much as the sight of South's legs jerking and tail thrashing.

Worse still was the inertness. South, motionless on the concrete floor, blood trickling out from a gash between its legs.

Its brother.

ITS BROTHER.

The Bear surged forward, fresh sorrow converted into fury and converted again into sheer power. North dug its claws into the undercarriage of the cop car. It dead lifted five thousand pounds of steel and iron up over its head and slammed the car back down on its roof.

What was left of the windshield came loose. The safety wiring between the front seat and the back seat bent, twisted, and came apart. Jack ripped his arm open on a jagged edge. Luke flopped bonelessly onto a bed of broken glass.

And then they were rising up again, playthings of momentum as the Bear roared and hoisted the cruiser overhead. Jack felt weightless for a moment. He groped to grab onto something. Anything.

He found nothing.

They came back down and all the weight came crashing back. Jack bounced with all the elasticity of a slab of cement. The wind exploded from his lungs. His vision went dim.

Somewhere above them, cutting through the white noise in his skull, the Bear roared. Claws stabbed through the undercarriage-turned-ceiling of the upturned cruiser. The steel peeled back with a protesting scream of meta;, the car shrieking against its own disembowelment.

Jack's sight cleared in time to see North staring down at him. The brown Bear streaked with white dust, black oil, and red blood. Foam bubbled and its snarling jaws. Its remaining eye bulged to bursting with rage.

It dug into the car, reaching for Jack like he was honeycomb in a beehive.

Jack crawled back away from the questing claws. His hand fell over Luke's limp wrist, but there was nothing else to do for him, Jack kept scrambling. He crawled out through the smashed window and staggered to his feet.

Sheer luck had put the overturned cruiser between him and the Bear. It was not a plan. Not strategy. Not even out of fear for his life. Jack had given up on his life. This thing was going to kill him. The certainty of it branded his every heartbeat a lie.

North bellowed and kicked the cruiser out of the way. The cop car screeched across the cement, clearing the path between the Bear and Jack.

Jack turned and ran. He wasn't getting away, no chance. All he was doing was buying seconds- seconds between him and that mouthful of fangs and rancid, raw meat breath.

Behind him, the sound of thunder coming. The Bear roared.

Don't look. Just don't look.

Of its own volition, his head twisted on the aching back.

Jesus Christ, why?

There was nothing to see over his shoulder. Nothing except the oncoming mountain of the Bear. Its paw was already cocked back, a paw as big around as a motorcycle tire, primed to come down and swat his head off his shoulders. Sometimes you're the windshield, but this time Jack Galindo was the bug.

Then the Bear went down.

North slipped. The Bear's padded foot came down in a pool of oil from the smashed cruiser and the creature simply lost traction. For a brief moment, the giant monstrosity became a circus bear. It wind-milled for balance, and then it did a full somersault and finished on its paws and knees.

Jackie Galindo reversed course at the same moment. Instinct had told him to run away, but now instinct compelled him to turn around and pit one hundred and sixty pounds of stringy meat and fragile bone up against the unrelenting, awesome bulk of the Omega Predator.

Because it had tripped.

Jackie jumped on the Bear's back. He hooked one arm around a neck as thick around as his torso.

North roared. It pistoned back up. *So fucking strong.* Jackie held on tighter, knowing that it wouldn't be long before the Bear flung him to the ground and dashed him open. His free hand went to his remaining piercing, the devil's head with its forked tongue and the curved horns. He almost had it when, North swung sharply to the left. Jackie flailed and nearly flew off entirely. His hand twisted into the bear's pelt and held on with everything he had.

His other hand went back to his ear. There was no time to undue the stopper. Jackie ripped the piercing right out of his fucking ear and drove it into the dark pit of North's remaining eye. He shoved it in horns first, and the piercing ripped that dark bubble wide open and sent it pouring down the Bear's snout in a dark gusher.

North howled. It twisted and Jack went flying off its shoulders- a headfirst ten-foot drop with a little extra speed from the wrenching torque of the Bear. Jack stuck an arm out to protect his head. He successfully prevented a skull fracture; but four of his fingers snapped under the initial impact with the concrete. Then his elbow broke as the weight of his entire body came down on it. His arm crumped and Jack came down hard on his shoulder. His collarbone shattered in an expanding shockwave of cracking bone.

Jack tumbled over landed flat on his back in a graying haze of shock. North's screeching agony was the only thing that kept him conscious.

The Bear swung blindly. Claws whistled through the air. North stomped in circles, shaking its head, fanning out droplets of blood from its ruined eyes. It roared, spraying spittle in every direction.

Jack tried to sit up and immediately convulsed back down. His entire left side was pure agony. He couldn't lift it all.

Biting his lip against the pain, Jack pushed himself along the floor with his feet, though even that felt like dragging his body through broken glass. He hissed out a breath, struggling not to scream.

North stopped fighting the air.

Slowly, the Bear swung its head in his direction. The shredded meat of its eyes stared right through him.

…North couldn't see, but it could hear.

Jack clamped his mouth shut even as his broken arm kept gnawing at him and hot blood ran down his face from his split ear. He didn't whimper. He didn't even breathe.

The Bear's nostrils expanded.

No, Jack begged. His eyes bulged. He still didn't dare make a sound. *Please. No, no, no.*

The Bear stepped towards him, led by its questing nose.

In the darkness inside its skull, North held on to the scent. The sister-killer's stench was now the only light

North knew. With every step the Bear took, that black light felt closer.

Closer.

North had a sound to go with the scent now, the rapid pitter-patter of the sister-killer's heart. The Bear groped forward with its claws. Scent and sound were almost overwhelming. The soft Meatflesh was close now. It had to be.

A swarm of hot gnats settled into its back. A brief roar drowned out the sound the sound of the sister-killer's heartbeat.

Luke pumped another round into the shotgun. He fired again. The 12 gauge round struck North square between the shoulders, but the blast did nothing but goad the Bear into swinging around towards him.

Luke squeezed the trigger. He aimed higher. Buckshot riddled North's skull.

The Bear roared. It lumbered through the darkness in the direction of the biting gnats. The ones that, even then, struck it in the chest.

Oh shit, Luke thought. *Oh shit.* The shotgun boomed in his hands and he immediately pumped in another round.

How many more shots are in this thing? Five? Twenty?

None?

He shot off another blast, right into the creature's chest.

It did nothing.

"Luke, GO!" Jack screamed.

Yes, run! Leave him! GO!

Instead, Luke pumped in another round.

The Bear was bleeding, bloody red specks in the thick fur of its chest and head, but it kept coming, blindly pursuing the reek of gunpowder. It passed underneath the raised auto-lift. Its ears brushed the bottom curve of the elevated cruiser's tires.

Luke raised the shotgun up and aimed for the bear's head. He pulled the trigger. Buckshot hit its head in a cloud. A fang chipped. Pellets lodged themselves in the Bear's ear. Buckshot pelted its skull, but nothing pierced the thick dome of its cranium.

Still more pellets from the widening spray missed Norths' head completely and struck the auto lift above the Bear's head. Lead shot ripped open the hydraulic tubing running along the lift column. Viscous orange fluid sprayed everywhere.

As the hydraulic fluid ran out, the lift, and the cop car perched on top of it, began to descend.

Slowly at first, and then faster and faster as more fluid ran out from the powershaft.

In its blind darkness, North never even knew what hit it. An unknown weight came down like God's hammer, buckling the Bear's formidable bones, driving it to its knees and then pressing down on its head. Harder. Harder.

Before North knew what was happening, even the darkness was gone.

27

Luke's face felt wet. He put his fingers to his temple, and they came back gray.

Gray.

Just like the pulped brains squeezing through the Bear's cracked skull.

And out of its' mouth.

It's still not dead, Luke thought. *The Bear's playing dead. Ha. Ha. Ha.*

He pumped the shotgun and pointed it at the creature pinned underneath the lift platform. He pulled the trigger.

Click.

Empty! Luke staggered back, putting as much distance as he could between himself and the creature's prone carcass. *It knows I'm out of ammo!* He fell to all fours and crawled away. He looked over his shoulder, certain that any moment now the Bear would rise up-

"Luke," Jack groaned. He tried to sit up, but his smashed arm screamed. Jack screamed in harmony.

"Jack!" Luke dropped the gun and broke into a run. His foot kicked one of the dead Bear's paws, but Luke never even looked down. He reached Jack's side and hovered over him, eager to do *something*, but not sure where he should start. Blood gushed down Jack's face from an ear that looked like it was split in half.

And his arm. Oh my fucking God, look at his arm.

Jack's arm was so twisted up, it looked like a fucking corkscrew.

Luke knelt down beside him. He gingerly tried to get his arms underneath Jack without jostling… Jesus, without jostling anything.

"Just do it," Jack hissed. He closed his eyes and clenched his teeth.

Luke did the same thing. Closed his eyes, clenched his teeth, and…

Oh, fuck.

He wrapped Jack in a *(ha, ha)* bear hug and hoisted him up.

Jack screamed. The sound bounced off the concrete walls, somehow becoming more tormented with every reverberation.

Luke tried to block it out. He focused on the wall. The plain, concrete wall that was just ten of the longest feet away that Luke had ever seen. He half-carried, half-dragged Jack along every one of them. All the while, Jack kept screaming in his ear. Not obscenities, not even words, just the primal agony of his smashed bones grinding together. Luke heard it all, right in the mixing booth. He tried to block it out.

Just keep going… Just keep going…

At last, they reached the wall. Luke did his best to set Jack down easy, for all the good it did. For Jack, every inch he was lowered felt like it was over hot coals. Finally, his butt touched down and he slumped against the wall. The pain didn't leave, but it settled at a lower level. Jack sat there with his head hung low, sucking in breath while hot blood and cold sweat mingled against his skin.

"Where…" Jack panted, "Where did you get the machine gun?"

"Oh," Luke said. He shrugged. "It was in the Jeep."

"And where… did you get a Jeep?"

Luke laughed. "Call it spoils of war."

"Last question. Who dressed you like my dad?"

Luke glanced down, realizing, seemingly for the first time, that someone had clad him in a flannel shirt and Wal-Mart jeans.

"Here's a better question," Luke replied. "Who thought it was a good idea to hook us up with the world's most fucked up petting zoo?"

"You did!" Jack shouted, but he was laughing too. Every chuckle was fresh rock salt in his fucked up arm, but he couldn't help it.

"Oh, no!" Luke was turning red, the way he always did when something cracked him up but he was struggling not to show it. "Don't you put this on me. You know what I wanted to do? I wanted to take you to a beach house and then let it 'slip' to the right Instagrams where you were going to be. Boom! Everybody feels better and nobody has to sleep in a car or get chased by a fucking Devil-Gator!"

"Yeah, but who would want to listen to that concept album?"

"Me," Luke said. He sat down beside Jack. "That album sounds fan-fucking-tastic. I think we should start researching it as soon as I renegotiate your contract."

"With Geffen?" Jack asked.

"With me. All of a sudden, I'm feeling significantly underpaid."

"I'm sure we can work something out," Jack said. He used his good arm to swipe blood away from his mouth so he stopped tasting it every time he spoke. "The least you deserve is a Saving My Life bonus. Or a Hard Ass incentive."

Luke let his head roll back against the wall. He exhaled slow and deep.

"Don't think you can sweet talk me and fog up the math, Jack. I'm smarter than you."

"Of course you are," Jack said. "You're better looking too."

"Damn right I am."

"Certainly a better dresser."

"Fuck yourself," Luke said. With some effort, he hauled himself back to his feet. "I'm going to find a phone- get us some cops and get you a doctor and a manicurist. Are you going to be alright by yourself?"

Jack nodded. The pain was monstrous, but it had steadied. Jack could take it. Indeed, just the knowledge that he was able to take it was better than a shot of morphine.

…Maybe.

"Jack?"

Jack snapped back to reality. "I'll manage," he said. "Go."

"Two minutes," Luke said. "Three if you want me to get you a Coke."

Jack watched him go. Luke was clearly hurting too. He spat blood as he dragged his left foot behind him, and he kept rotating his right shoulder as he walked. But there was no hiss of discomfort and none of the theatrics that Jack associated with Luke's frequent "racquet ball injuries." This guy walking it off in jeans and flannel was tougher than that.

"Hey, Luke," Jack said.

"Yeah?"

Jack winced, but made himself sit up straighter.

"Last track on that concept album… *The Man Makes the Clothes.*"

Luke blanched. "Come on, Jack. You're supposed to be a rock star. That pop-country piss ain't gonna fit."

Jack grinned. "OK. If you think it's a no-go, then never mind."

"He listens! Finally!"

With that, Luke was gone.

28

The reception area looked even worse now. It had already been bad then, what with the cop on the floor with his face ripped off, but the addition of a second body, head practically dangling between her shoulder blades, did nothing for the decor. It was like a reminder that things could always get worse.

Not anymore tonight they can't. You're finding a phone and then you're getting the fuck out of here, free and clear.

And, like the universe seeking to assure him, there was a phone right there by the double doors. It lay amongst the other detritus that had spilled from the dead woman's purse. Even better, it had landed outside the spreading pool of the woman's blood.

Luke tried to not break down crying as he went for it. He couldn't bring himself to step through the bloody moat separating him and the phone, but by standing to the side of the door and leaning all the way over, he thought he would just be able to reach it.

He could. The glass face of the screen felt like cool water against his fingertips. He stretched just a little further, just far enough to get a good grip on the phone.

The glass double doors opened. A blue, webbed hand closed around Luke's questing wrist. The rough skin surrounded his hand with the bitter cold of the Marianas Trench. The shock of that cold robbed Luke of the single breath he could have used to warn Jack. Before he got another one, that hand pulled him through the door out into the night and a second hand closed tight over his nose and mouth, filling his head with scent of saltwater and rotting fish.

"There you are," she said. "I was hoping I'd see you again."

It was the last thing West said before the Shark completely wiped away her Meatface.

29

Slumped against the wall, Jack did his best to stay conscious. Some dim, soft-spoken corner of his mind insisted it was important he stay awake. *Comas,* it cautioned. At the moment, Jack had no idea what a coma even was, but he gathered they were not good.

The pain in his shattered arm had helped at first, but that entire arm was turning swollen and numb (and also a little bit black). As the pain faded, he caught himself drifting off. One time, he almost drifted completely asleep before the scream of a coyote startled him back to consciousness.

Was it a coyote? Are you sure?

That thought didn't last long. It was too obtuse for his clouded mind to hold onto. Soon, his eyelids fluttered shut again. He drifted. Then snapped awake just as quickly. He slapped himself with his good arm, but the blow didn't have nearly enough sting on it. This wasn't working. He needed something that really hurt.

Of course, the first thought that came to mind was Tracy.

Now there's an idea! You want to get hurt? Do you remember Costa Rica?

Of course he remembered Costa Rica. He and Tracy rented a villa overlooking the Monteverde Cloud Forest. It was the rainy season, and they spent the entire week lying naked in a hammock under a bamboo awning. Seven blissful days making love, sharing tequila, and murmuring rough draft song lyrics in each other's ears.

Oh, you're awake now with that razor blade spinning in your chest, aren't ya? Here, have one more to grow on. What about Texas? You remember Texas, right?

Of course he did. That was only six months ago. Right before he fucked everything up. The show

was grueling. Two full sets and then four encores, the last two of them unplanned.

Far above, he hears them still screaming his name, but he has nothing left to give them. He's exhausted. His

*body's aching and his face paint's a
ruined, streaky mess that makes his skin
burn like hell. He doesn't know what
plans the rest of the band has, and he
doesn't care. All he wants to do is wash
off the makeup and get out of the black
leather that reeks of stage smoke. Then
he wants a Tecate from the fridge and
he wants to zone out with something
stupid on Netflix.*

*He opens the door and Tracy's
waiting for him on the couch. Tracy,
lounging in yoga pants and a baggy t-
shirt. The familiarity should make
seeing her routine, but it isn't. It never
is. Every time he sees her, it's like he's
discovered something beautiful and
perfect and completely, utterly brand
new*

*He goes to her. He sits down on the
couch, and she pushes him flat on his
back without so much as a word. Her
fingers trace the sides of his ribcage
and run up along his neck. It feels like
the only parts of him that exist are the
parts underneath her fingertips.*

*He touches her sides underneath the
t-shirt, going around her hips and
settling on the small of her back. She*

leans low, bringing her lips towards his. Then she stops just short of his mouth.

"Not yet," she whispers.

She goes to the makeup table and comes back with a moist cloth. She wipes the makeup off his face, dabbing away at the green and black until there's nothing left but the skin he was born with.

Then, and only then, does she kiss him.

"There's my handsome lover," she murmurs against his lips.

Glass shattered. Something large and dark flew through one of the windows in the roll-up door. It swooped down on him in a flurry of motion.

Jack threw his arms up to shield his face, a movement that awoke primordial agony in his ruined arm, but he had no time to do anything else as the thing…

Never came.

Jack heard nothing. No snarls. No running feet. Just the howling of the desert wind.

Slowly, Jack lowered his hands.

He saw the broken window. And he saw the thing that had come through it. It lay there on the floor. Not a monster, just a pitiful, ruined carcass of a victim.

But it can't be Luke, Jack thought. *I saw him just a minute ago and he was fine. Bloody and beat to hell, but he was okay. Shit, he walked out of here like the king of the world. It can't be Luke.*

Luke still has his legs.

Jack kept staring at the broken thing with tied-off rags around the stumps where its legs used to be. He looked at the thing with Luke's hair and Luke's face and waited for it to somehow not be Luke.

The thing opened Luke's eyes then. It made a muffled moan with Luke's voice.

No kidding himself now. Jack hauled himself up and rushed to his friend's side.

"Luke!" Jack screamed. "Luke!"

Luke hacked and convulsed. He clawed at his throat. Jack reached into Luke's mouth. His fingers hooked at something hard and sharp-edged deep in Luke's throat and pulled it loose.

Blood came out with it; great, hacking spatters of it landed on Luke's chest.

Jack tried to get him to sit up. He mopped frothy blood from Luke's lips.

"Come on," Jack pleaded. "Slow down. Just breathe, Luke."

Luke cleared another gusher of blood. "I'm sorry, Jack," he said. "I'm so sorry."

"What happened to you?" Jack screamed.

Except he already knew. Of course he knew.

North, South, and East were dead.

West was not.

Luke grabbed Jack's arm with surprising strength.

"I tried not to tell her," Luke gasped. "I tried to lie." His bloody lips trembled. "But she always knew… and every time I lied, she ate another piece of me."

Jack tried to pick him up, putting all of Luke's weight on his ruined arm and not even feeling it. "Come on, we have to get out of here before she-"

Luke squeezed him tighter.

"She's already gone, Jack! I told her what she wanted to know and now she wants you to follow her!"

"Told her what!? Where's she going!?"

"Tracy, Jack!" Luke screamed. "She's going after Tracy!"

...No.

His first feeling was not panic. Not fear. It was more like, *Snip.* Luke spoke Tracy's name and Jack floated away.

No. Just... No. She wouldn't even know where to find Tracy.

"I'm sorry, Jack," Luke repeated. Blood leaked steadily down his face now. More oozed from the ragged stumps of his knees. "She said that she'll wait for you... but not for long. She said to make sure you hurry or she'll.... she'll..." Luke went limp in Jack's arms. He might have been dead, were it not for the cringing shame still alive in his eyes. "Four times and I wouldn't tell her anything. She took my feet and my knees and I didn't tell her, but then... Oh Jesus, I just couldn't take it again."

It's not your fault.

I'm the one who made you come out here.

Nobody could have gone through what you did.

That's what Jack thought, but couldn't say. The words were trapped by the clamps tightening around his throat.

"I'm so sorry, Jack," Luke wheezed. His voice was a ghost of a whisper. His eyes were sinking in his head. Pulling away.

Jack shook him.

He screamed in Luke's face.

He raged and cried and demanded Luke hold on.

Jack did none of those things. He held Luke and just waited.

"I'm…"

Luke was gone.

30

Jack was not. Jack was still on his knees with Luke in his arms. Against his will, he pictured Tracy out there in the night, still sleeping and completely unaware as West hurtled towards her.

Luke would have sent West to the beach house in Malibu. Even driving fast, that's four hours away.

More cops would be at the station long before then. Somebody would have to come. They could reach out to Malibu PD and have Tracy ushered somewhere safe long before West ever reached the coast.

If the cops believed him.

If they wanted to hear a single word he had to say with dead bodies all over the place.

Including the two cops that brought you in in the first place.

There would be a lot of questions before the police would even consider sending anyone anywhere on his say-so.

He could call 911 and leave an anonymous message. Tell them that someone was coming to kill Tracee Trance.

And get dismissed as a crackpot before you even finished talking. Even if someone did drive by as a precaution, how long would they stay? Fifteen minutes? Ten?

And without knowing what West was, it didn't matter who Tracy had with her. West would tear them apart.

That left Jack.

Which is exactly what West wants.

And she was going to get it. No questions, no hesitation. No matter what had changed between them, there was one thing that hadn't. He would die for Tracy.

Die with her, you mean.

Yes, fine. Die with her. That was the truth, wasn't it? Half dead, one-armed Jack wasn't the calvalry. He was just company.

He needed keys. Luke had mentioned a Jeep. Jack thought first of searching his pockets, he braced himself to go rooting through his best friend's corpse.

And then he remembered the rough, jagged obstruction he'd pulled out of Luke's throat.

Luke's keys still lay in the pool of blood where Jack had thrown them.

Reluctantly, Jack settled Luke back to the floor. He wiped the blood from his friend's face as best he could.

"Nothing's your fault," Jack whispered. His cracked, wretched voice echoed in the tomb of the garage. "I wished I'd told you that when you could hear me, but I'm sure I'll get another chance soon."

Soon as you walk through Tracy's front door probably, a small voice insisted.

Keys in hand, he staggered out to the parking lot, and discovered two more arguments against waiting for more cops to arrive; arguments with their heads ripped off and their insides strewn across the asphalt.

The Jeep waited a little further out, parked crooked with one wheel up on the curb. Jack limped towards it.

Limping towards death. There's a single.

He pressed on, like a beaten dog
returning to its abusive master. Steam
rose from the hot blood coating his
face. His ripped up calve had opened
again. Blood leaked behind his every
step. His smashed fingers were swollen
and bent like bananas. His whole arm
had turned into a gnarled tree branch.

He came to the Jeep and finally
admitted to himself what he'd already
seen waiting for him on the hood.

Boots. Boots with the bitten off feet
still inside of them. And a pair of jean-
wrapped casings that had once been
legs from the knees down.

He swept Luke's legs off of the
Jeep. And here, something else to
discover. There was no more fear or
disgust left in him. It occurred to him,
almost as an afterthought, that those
emotions were only for people who still
thought they could survive.

Jack got into the Jeep and started
the engine. He pulled onto the highway.
The road ahead of him was dark,
empty, and, to Jack, short. The highway
no longer stretched out to infinity in
Jack's mind. It ran only as far as a
beach house in Malibu. His road ended

there. Tracy's road ended there.
Everything ended there.

Jack got the Jeep up to speed.

31

You can judge a woman's true beauty by how she looks when she's sleeping. There's no makeup to hide imperfections. There's no posing or angling towards her "good side." There's only exactly who she is when she's at her most unaware and vulnerable.

By that metric, Tracy Stanton, better known as Tracee Trance, was stunning. The sheets were pulled back, revealing a body covered by nothing but a tank top and boy shorts and leaving no doubt that there was no wardrobe or photoshop trickery behind her high breasts, flat abs, and exquisitely sculpted legs. A single ray of sunlight arrowed through the window and framed her face perfectly. Her blonde hair seemed to glow in its light. Even sleeping, her lips pressed together in a maddeningly kissable bow.

It was fitting to find her in a bed, because to look at her was to look upon a dream made into flesh.

And then the alarm went off and Tracy opened her eyes. They were bloodshot and hazy, like smog over a sky of purest blue.

She threw up a little. Not a lot. She wiped at it with the back of her hand, spat on the pillow, and groped for her cellphone. She poked the screen. She slid her finger across it. Nothing happened. The

BLEEP! BLEEP!

of the alarm continued unabated. She set the phone down and turned her attention to the pile of pills on her nightstand. She mashed two of them to powder with her fist and snorted up as much of the gritty dust as she could.

The effects were immediate. Now she could focus. With her head clear, she understood that it was not her phone sounding the alarm, it was the security box by the front door. The one that informed her someone was at the gate.

She made her way down the hall into the living room. The guy was still there. Jimmy or Javier or whatever the fuck his name was. He was sprawled out naked in front of the fireplace, both of their clothes strewn on the floor around him. Tracy kicked him in the thigh as she walked past. He came awake with a snort.

"If I wanted you to stay the night, I would have let you sleep in the bed," she said.

"You drove," he muttered. He tried to caress her calf as she passed. Tracy kept walking, right across his pants.

"Hey!" He sat up. "Those are eight hundred dollar jeans!"

Tracy rolled her eyes. "I'll buy you ten."

You got Jack those same jeans for his birthday last year. He smiled and told you that was an awful lot of money to pay for something that was going to soak up crotch sweat all day.

Tracy pushed that voice aside. Jack wouldn't recognize something valuable if it walked up and stomped on his balls.

Tonalist barked at her from his bed in the corner. The little Havanese stood on rigid legs and yipped incessantly in the direction of the door.

Poor little guy needed to be fed. Tracy made a note to fill his bowl as soon as she finished taking out the trash.

She punched in the code to turn off the alarm and open the gate. "Your Uber's here. Get your seven hundred and ninety-eight dollar jeans and get out. Don't call me, I'll call you."

Javier or Jimmy was still fussing over his pants. "I didn't call an Uber."

She rolled her eyes. "I don't care what startup you're pushing. They're here."

The French doors exploded inward a shower of glass. Tonalist whimpered and scurried away from the door. Tracy screamed and leapt back as the blonde woman rushed inside.

She came quickly. So quickly that all Tracy could get were glimpses as she swept forward. Lithe muscles. Wild eyes framed by a tangle of unwashed hair. White teeth bared in a face of tanned, skin. Taut, naked flesh.

And ferocity. Sheer, unrelenting ferocity.

Jimmy/Javier bounded to his feet. He threw his jeans at the blonde wild woman, eyes wide with terror, like she wasn't twenty pounds lighter than him. "Get back!" he screamed. "Get the fuck away from me-"

The crazy woman grabbed him by the throat. She lifted Jimmy/Javier up off his feet and slammed him down on his head. His skull cracked open against the floor, drenching Tracy's white carpet with red.

Tracy screamed. She twisted towards the open door. She took a step towards the sun.

Fingers like talons snared her hair. Fingers hot and sticky with blood. Tracy was pulled off her feet, swung around in a disorienting loop, and thrown onto the couch. The naked blonde pounced on her. She straddled Tracy's hips and forced her head back.

"Oh God," Tracy moaned. "Oh God, oh God, oh-"

"STOP IT!" Her attacker roared.

Tracy stopped. She stopped everything. Speaking. Breathing. Blinking.

The blonde woman seemed to lose sight of her for a moment. Her flat, inhuman eyes turned towards something only she could see. Something a million years in the past.

Oh God, Oh God, Oh God.

"Don't say that," West whispered. "There are no others. They're gone… it's only me now."

The blonde's eyes came back to the present them. They came back brimming with fury.

West got off of her. She surveyed her surroundings. The furniture. The small, fluffy dog trembling with his tail between his legs in the corner. The gas fireplace, currently cold and dark. The picture window showcasing Tracy's private stretch of the Pacific Ocean.

And, lastly, the small hill of cocaine on the coffee table. The base of the white mound was littered with pills, like relics left on an ancient beach by a forgotten civilization.

At the sight of it, West discovered that her siblings weren't as gone as she thought. Her reaction to the hill of drugs was classic East. Little sister East, who always took such delight in taunting the prey in their Meat Language.

"Jesus," West said. "You're the girl Jack's on suicide watch for? I thought he was down to earth."

Something clicked in Tracy's head then. Something that tied Jack, cocaine, and strangers barging into her house all together. There were some parts that didn't fit, like the intruder's nudity and the dull ache in her scalp, but it made some kind of sense and that was good. More than sense, it made her *mad* and that was even better.

"Wait a minute," she said. "Wait one fucking minute." She stood up. "Did *Jack* send you here? Oh my fucking god. Get out of my house right now. And you tell Jack that if he ever sends another fucking intervention, deprogrammer... *whatever the fuck you are,* then I will actually kill him. And you're going to pay for my door or-"

West slapped her. It was the first time in her entire life that anyone had laid a hand on Tracy Stanton or Tracee Trance, and she was more astounded than hurt.

"…You're fired," she gasped. "Whatever halfway house you work for, tell them to make you up a bed because-"

West slapped her again. Hard enough this time to rock her head to the side and draw blood from the corner of her mouth.

"Have you checked on your friend?" West asked. "Have you actually looked at him?"

Tracy saw him then. Really saw what they'd done to *(Jackson. His name was Jackson.)*. Gray brain tissue oozed from the fissure in his shattered skull. The pool of blood around him was the size of a throw rug.

West closed the gap between herself and Tracy. She stood so they were eye to eye.

"Don't speak again," West said. "There's nothing you need to say."

Her teeth.

"Sit," West said. "Wait."

Oh Jesus… her teeth.

"Do not."

This isn't real. I got dosed. They gave me LSD, not Oxy.

"Run."

I'll close my eyes and this will all be gone.

Tracy squeezed her eyes shut. She scrunched them together so tightly, even tears couldn't escape.

She opened them again and the blonde was still there. And she still looked the same. She still had flat, black eyes and a mouth crowded with sharp, triangular teeth that pushed her lips back in a permanent snarl.

Her lips suddenly pulled back even further, exposing another dozen farm combine teeth.

It was a smile.

"This was right."

"W-w-what? What's right?" Tracy asked.

"You'll hurt him."

"What are you talking about!?" Tracy shrieked. "I don't understand! What do you want from me!?"

In truth, West wasn't entirely sure what she wanted. Not in Meat Words anyway. She understood pain, though, and on some primal level she understood that the pain of losing her family could not be repaid with simple teeth and claws.

Yet, the image of Jack Galindo driving through the night, pushing the limits of his smashed Meat Body and knowing, all along, that he was only coming to watch her die…

That felt closer to even.

32

For the first time in his life, Jack actually drove at the speed limit.

It was the fastest his devastated body would allow. He could only drive with one hand, a hand that wouldn't stop shaking no matter how hard he tried. His other arm, the shattered one, he had propped in the open window. The support of the frame was the closest thing to comfort for the ruined limb.

That was one reason for his steady pace. The other reason was that he couldn't risk getting pulled over. One look at him and the cops would have him tied up for hours.

And you wouldn't want to be late for your own closed casket funeral, would you?

Jack let that voice have its say. He was going to die. Tracy too. He knew that. Different variations of the same thought had plagued him all through the dark night.

Every breath you take is sand from an hourglass.

This car is being driven by a dead man.

What if she gives you a chance to talk to Tracy first? What will you say to her?

You're going to die.

She's going to die.

Execution by Evisceration.

It went on and on. He drifted along with those voices tormenting him until the first purple light of dawn rose over the mountains.

Was it then that the voices began to bleed together into background noise? Or perhaps it came as he reached the fabled Pacific Coast Highway, just as the sky truly began to turn orange? Yes, maybe it was then that the voices were swallowed up by the hum of tires and the wind whipping past his open window finally started to whisper to him like it used to. Not in words, but in chords. C sus, D major and C major. Thunder out of the clear purple and orange sky.

Jack's foot pressed down a little harder. He pushed the Jeep up to 70.

The wind came faster. The whispers grew louder.

West's trap. That's what he was supposed to be walking into. West, who looked like a USC spring break goddess but was really…

I don't even know what she is, he realized. All he knew was what she'd done to Luke. She was undoubtedly terrible. She was a monster like East and the others. She was fangs and fury and unrelenting power.

….But she doesn't know what I am either.

He goosed the Jeep a little more, and the roaring engine agreed with him. *She* was setting the trap? He'd gone up against the Mountain Lion, the Bear, and the Alligator and he was still standing.

She was the one setting a trap? For *him?*

"Bitch shouldn't have given up the element of surprise," he muttered. "She needed it."

And then Jackie Galindo surprised himself by laughing out loud. Once he started, he found that he was unable to stop, and his laughter mixed with the

roar of the engine as the Jeep crossed
from the desert and out into the blue
embrace of the Pacific Ocean.

<u>33</u>

At the same time that West was ruining Tracy's rug in Malibu, record store clerk Miles Lemire slumped over the counter at Scratched CDs in Sylmar and cursed the son of a bitch who insisted that 8 AM was an acceptable time for a used music store to be open for business.

There was no reason for him to be there at this hour. Zero. None. Nobody came looking for *Countdown to Extinction* at 8 o'clock in the fucking morning. Nobody went next door for a kale and who gives a fuck smoothie and then popped in to fill a gap in their Alice Cooper archives. If they got more than two customers before 11 AM, that was cause to drop the confetti.

Of course, opening at 8 wasn't really a business decision. Just like it wasn't a business decision to make Miles open the store.

No, the real reason he was here wasn't economics. It was that his father (also known as "the boss," also known as "the son of a bitch") insisted that the early morning start time brought badly needed "structure" to Miles' life.

Behind his closed lids, Miles rolled his eyes. His life was structured just fine- get off work, get drunk, see bands, go to work, repeat.

Except maybe last night he'd gone just *a little* too hard on the drinking. Maybe. A little.

He checked his phone. 8:35 AM. At the very least, he really ought to unlock the door. His father would be swinging by any minute "just to check in," and he was already going to have plenty to say about the reek of whiskey on Miles' clothes and his long hair hanging loose instead of in a ponytail, "like we agreed." Honestly, how somebody so establishment owned a music store, Miles would never know.

Still, own it he did, and if the store wasn't open when he came by, he might dock an hour's pay, and Miles couldn't have that. Not when his solo album was almost a quarter funded.

…But he was so goddamn hungover. And more than a little

nauseous. And seriously, fuck your "structure," dad.

Fuck all of it, he decided. *I don't need this job. And I don't need your shitty basement apartment either.* He let his head roll along the countertop, like the dirty wood veneer was a pillow he could settle more comfortably into.

Fuck it, he reiterated. Let the door stay locked.

Knock.

Knock.

…No. It couldn't be.

Knock.

Knock.

It was.

Someone rapping, as of someone gently tapping, at the motherfucking door.

At motherfucking 8:35 AM.

Well, too goddamn bad. Miles' Rock and Roll Rebel was up now. Let them keep walking.

The knocker persisted. A drumbeat nobody asked for.

Knock.

Knock.

"Jesus Christ," Miles muttered to himself. Then, not to himself, "We're closed!" And then he winced. Even his own voice hurt his head.

Knock.

Knock.

Miles couldn't see the persistent son of a bitch, not with the shelving unit of concert DVDs between the cash register and the door, but he had a mental image nonetheless. A perfect artist's rendition of some sixteen-year-old shithead who thought Green Day counted as old school punk; some fat, pompous, know-nothing kid cutting class and looking for a place to kill an hour.

Well, try Hot Topic, junior.

Junior did not try Hot Topic. Junior, incredibly, just kept fucking knocking.

"I said we're closed!" Miles roared. "Fuck off!"

It wasn't the hangover headache squeezing his temples now. It was anger. The same anger that had gotten him fired by every boss that wasn't his father. It was the sudden boiling point that always came on him without warning. Just like that, the kid was on his last warning. There wasn't going to be another one.

Knock.

Miles stormed out from behind the counter. He knocked over a mug of discount band pins and scattered Sex Pistols, Journey, and Iron Maiden logos across the counter.

"Better check a mirror, fuckface." Miles swore. He came around the corner of the shelving unit in a fast march, his fists knotted at his side. "If you don't see Ozzy Osbourne looking back at you, then get ready to see my fist smashing your fucking teeth out!"

…Miles stopped. His scowl fell apart like a cheap piece of furniture.

He gaped at the door. Not because he didn't recognize the person on the other side of the glass. But because he did. Miles one hundred percent knew exactly who it was. He just refused to believe that… *HE* was standing outside of Scratched CDs.

Knocking. Waiting to be let in.

Miles scurried over. From furious to solicitous in less than two seconds.

The customer pushed open the door. "Thanks for opening up," he said. "I know I'm not Ozzy."

Miles had nothing to say. There was still too much to be processed. Not just the reality of… *HIM*, but the reality of the shape that HE was in. The whole side of his face was caked in dried blood. More of it ran wild across his clothes in herds of spatter patterns.

And then there was his arm. If Miles weren't still in shock, he might have puked just from looking at it.

That's an arm that's never going to play guitar again, Miles thought. And then quickly clamped down because to even think such a thing was heresy.

The customer brushed past him. He walked with a limp, but didn't seem particularly bothered by it. He hobbled from one rack to the next, perusing old CDs just like customers did every day.

Except none of them leave a trail blood behind them as they walk.

And none of them are… HIM.

"You got *'Coronation of the Killers'*?" the customer asked.

"O… original or remastered?" Miles croaked.

"Either's fine."

Numbly, tripping over feet that didn't feel attached, Miles walked further down the stacks. He picked up a copy of the CD and took it to the cash register. He tried to punch the price into the register and screwed it up. And screwed it up again. His fingers wouldn't stop shaking long enough to put in the right price.

The man with his face on the album cover coughed. "I wouldn't worry about the register," he said. "I seem to have misplaced my wallet. You know, one of those nights."

He took a pen from beside the register and scribbled a few looping lines in the message book they kept next to the phone.

"I know that's not a credit card receipt," he said, "But it's my experience that anything with my name on it tends to go up in value."

He pushed the signed pad back towards Miles.

"You get my meaning?"

Miles didn't answer, transfixed by the scrawl of ink and blood, and the customer didn't wait for a response. He took his CD.

"Keep the change," he said.

And off he went. Miles only had a view of his back now; only saw ripped fabric and the bloody wounds beneath. The customer was going… going…

"Wait!" Miles screamed, just before the customer and his mysteries disappeared forever.

The customer stopped. Thank God, he stopped. He turned. Waited.

"I just…" Miles faltered. He lost his voice. Found it again.

"Are… are you him? I mean, are you… Are you really him?"

15 years of whiskey and cigarettes had been squeegeed from Mile's voice. He looked once more at the pad and confirmed that the name written there was truly the name that was written there.

"Are you really Jackie Galindo?"

The customer smiled, cracking the crust of dried blood around his lips and baring a mouthful of red-stained teeth in a vicious grin.

Miles knew then. He knew it without having to hear a single word.

The customer said it anyway.

"Yeah," Jackie said. "That's exactly who I am."

He raised his arm. Not the one holding the CD, the wreck that belonged to someone with a gambling problem and an impatient bookie, and sketched a salute Miles' way.

"Hold on to that autograph, it's about to triple in value." Jackie said. "Rockstars are never hotter than when they're cold."

And then he really was gone, leaving nothing behind but his name.

-   -   -

Back on the road, the 405 heading towards the 101, Jackie turned on the radio. No iPod or spotify here, and he was glad for it. Jackie Galindo didn't want Jack's carefully curated choir of mourners and wanderers. He wanted thunder. He wanted to be in the company of monsters.

And the Rock and Roll Gods obliged. KROQ, KLOS, JackFM. They were there no matter the station- AC/DC, Motorhead, Black Sabbath... he rode to Malibu with a chorus of demons and devils heralding his coming.

He was Rolling Thunder and Pouring Rain.

He was the Ace of Spades.

He. Was. Eye. Urn. Man.

It went on like that. All the way up until he pulled into Tracy's driveway just as one final song came on.

The Foo Fighters, *Times Like These*.

And Jackie Galindo threw his head back and laughed long and loud.

Still laughing, he shut off the Jeep and stepped out to meet his death.

34

West did not move. She sat opposite Tracy and kept her gaze fixed on the Grammy over the fireplace. (Not that she actually saw it. It just happened to be in her line of sight.) West didn't blink. She didn't speak. And there was only the slightest rise of her breasts to even hint that she was still breathing.

Tracy sobbed again. It happened on and off. Coming to grips with what her life had become was like trying to find a good place to grab a porcupine. Every attempt only netted a fresh burst of tears.

Slowly, West turned her head. Black eyes surveyed the weeping pop star while five hundred years of East's influence whispered in her ear.

"I'm sorry, Tracy," West said. "Here you are- no handlers, all of this unexpected stress. You must feel like hell. Is there anything I can do to help you… relax?"

Not trusting herself to speak, not with the hysterics pulsing behind her eyes, Tracy nodded.

"Not a problem," West said.

The blonde leaned towards the table. There was a mirror next to the mound of cocaine, but West ignored it and stuffed a tablespoon of powder into the snuffbox of her hand instead.

The hand still sticky with Jackson's blood.

West brought her hand up to Tracy's face. Her hand and the drugs. There was enough blood to turn the cocaine a pastel shade like strawberries.

Tracy went at it anyway without hesitation. She shook her head back and forth in the nook of West's hand, snorting loudly with both nostrils, intent on sucking up as much powder as she could.

When the powder was gone, and after she licked the residue off of West's knuckles, only then did Tracy ease back in her chair. A glassy sheen in her eyes cast a polish over the wracked terror that had quivered there only moments before.

Out of idle curiosity, West took a short sniff for herself.

Waited.

…Frankly, she didn't see the allure.

"Jack used this too?" she asked.

At the question, some shameful awareness came back into Tracy's eyes. She couldn't look West in the eye, but it wasn't fear that made Tracy avert her gaze.

West pounced on her with a glee that would have made East proud. She rubbed some of the gritty white powder between her fingers. "Jack didn't like this, did he?"

Unable to meet those gleeful, vicious eyes, Tracy shook her head. "No," she said.

"Did he ask you to stop?"

"…He did."

"And what did he do when you said you wouldn't?" West pressed.

Tracy couldn't even look at her. She kept her eyes cast down between her knees.

"Answer me," West said.

"He flushed my pills," Tracy whispered. "My coke. Everything. I threw him out. I told him to get out of my life and never come back."

West sat silently, absorbing the information. She tried to follow the Meat Logic of what Tracy had told her, forcing herself to think like one of them. It wasn't easy, but she followed it along past all of its contradictions and foolishness.

"You're going to die because of what he did," West said.

Tracy shot out of her chair. She did it without even thinking about it. She swung clumsily towards the door.

"*Sit,*" West said. She didn't even raise her voice. There was so much of the Shark in it, she didn't have to. Tracy obediently sank back down into the chair on quivering legs.

"You're going to die to punish him," West said. "Remember that when he gets here." She smiled, caught up in the throes of a creativity she'd never experienced before. "Make sure he knows that you blame him for what's going to happen to you. Say it to him right before I take your face off."

West's eyes turned black again. Looking into them was like looking into the ocean on a moonless night. Tracy recoiled as far into the couch as she could.

"What are you!?" she shrieked. "What the fuck are you!?"

"…Hungry," West said. But she wasn't looking at Tracy.

She was looking at Tonalist, looking at the corner where the dog huddled and tried to be as invisible as possible.

He was invisible no longer. West got up. Tracy watched the naked blonde saunter over to the little dog, the dog who had been just a puppy when she road tripped out to LA from Des Moines.

If she needed any more proof of how terrified she was, Tracy had it now. The proof of was in her silence as West reached out for the little Havanese and snared his collar in her dainty, tapered, bloody fingers.

The dog whimpered as West picked him up. He twisted and writhed in her grip to no avail. The blonde's mouth was first filled with broken-glass teeth again, and then it was *widening*. Her jaws creaked and groaned, revealing more teeth and darkness.

Tracy bit her knuckles to keep from screaming. *When will it stop?*

But she knew when it would stop-when the blonde… *freak's* jaws were large enough to swallow her sweet little dog in a single bite. Her baby Tonalist, who never judged her or left her or did anything but love her always.

And Tracy couldn't even speak up to beg for his life.

West dangled the dog over her distended maw. Easily large enough now to swallow Tonalist whole. Tracy looked away. She closed her eyes and waited in darkness to hear her dog's final whimper.

She heard an electric guitar instead.

Slowly, Tracy opened her eyes. West stood in place, Tonalist still held above her head, but her black eyes swung from side to side, as if the chords swirling through the air left lighted tails for her to follow.

Somebody was playing a guitar at the back of the house.

"Is there another way in here?" the blonde asked through her gaping, distorted mouth.

Tracy forced herself to nod. "Around back. From the beach…. That's the way Jack always came in."

West's dark eyes somehow turned even blacker as the guitar only grew louder. The instrumental grew in power like gathering storm clouds. The notes rumbled through the floorboards.

"You're going to take me to him," West said. Only a whisper, but absolutely clear. "If you try to run, I'll find him myself. And I'll take what's left of you with me."

But first, West dropped Tonalist into her mouth. The crunching of the dog's bones was barely audible as the snarling guitar kicked up another notch.

35

Tracy led with West following close behind. West didn't have a hand on her. She didn't need to. She had hold of the singer's life, and that was enough to keep her in check. Tracy led her down a short hallway. The guitar was louder now, cranked up to the point of distortion. It made the doors vibrate in their frames.

West let Tracy lead on, even though there was no question where they were going now. The closed door directly at the end of the hall rattled the hardest. It bucked and trembled, like something on the other side was fighting to get out.

Tracy stopped just short of the door. Hesitantly, she put her hand to the handle.

Her conscience rose up briefly. *You're not really just going to hand him over, are you? Have you been seeing what I've been seeing?*

West poked her between the shoulder blades then. Her finger had become long and blue and the curved claw at the tip was sharp enough to draw blood.

Tracy opened the door without another thought. She stumbled inside with West close behind her.

And Jackie Galindo was there waiting for them.

He stood in the center of Tracy's meditation room; the soothing scenery of the Pacific at his back and her Buddhist reflection pool at his side. A statue of the Budda himself sat cross-legged atop a pillar in the center of the stone pool. Perhaps the marble effigy had some enlightened pacifist wisdom to impart to the room. If so, there was no hearing it over the swirling tornado building inside of the small room.

The music originated from the sound system next to the pool. Tracy normally used it to play Tibetan throat singing or Buddhist chants. Right now, it blasted out Jackie Galindo's instrumental track, *Death on Contact,* from his first platinum album, *Coronation of Killers.* Strictly an instrumental track, but Jackie considered it some of his finest work. Pure, distilled, molten iron pouring

285

forth for three minutes and thirteen seconds. Absolutely no words necessary.

The guitar shrieked on, filling the air with gathering storm clouds. Notes flew, coming in short strikes like throwing knives and then stretching out like the agonized wailing of victims on the torture rack.

Jackie stood in the center of it all. His brown eyes smoldered in his mask of blood. His good hand was knotted into a fist. His bad hand had turned black all the way up to the elbow.

West stared him down from the doorway. Her black eyes met his brown. Just like that, another force entered the room alongside the music. It kindled in the place where Jackie's eyes met West's. It hit like a tsunami running headlong into an H-Bomb blast, incomprehensible power against incomprehensible power.

The Buddha looked on. Serenely awaiting whatever happened next.

Jackie reached out with his good hand and cranked the stereo down. The song still screeched on, but not so

loudly that they couldn't hear each
other speak.

"Morning," Jackie said. "Hope you
don't mind me sneaking in through the
back. I don't really care if you do, but it
still seems like a nice thing to say."

At Tracy's side, the blonde stayed
perfectly motionless. It wasn't even
anger on her face. It was sheer,
emotionless blackness.

Jack-

No, that's not Jack

Jackie smiled in the face of the
abyss.

"Like the song?" he asked. "I would
have been happy to do the live version
for you, but I think my guitar playing
days are over." He shook the gnarled
remnants of his left hand in her
direction.

Never taking her eyes from
Jackie's, West's hand flashed out and
seized Tracy by the throat. West yanked
her forward and bent her over
backwards, almost as if they were
dancing. She forced Tracy's head back,
exposing the soft, white curve of her
throat. West's mouth rippled with

dozens of jagged teeth. She opened her jaws wide. Tracy screamed.

Jackie didn't flinch. West did not bring her teeth down for a killing bite. She held Tracy in place, feeling the pop star tremble in her arms. West could feel the singer's heartbeat through her skin. It danced at a frantic, unrelenting tempo.

And she could feel Jackie's. This close, she felt its vibration in the air. Slow. Steady. Completely unafraid.

Not what West wanted.

"Good call," Jackie said. "She's the only reason you're still alive."

West blinked. Had she mistaken the Meat Words?

She's the only reason you're still alive.

…No, she hadn't misunderstood.

West made a sound of own. A deep, sonorous, rhythmic pulse like a bilge pump.

She was laughing.

"Laugh if you want, but I'll be damned if I know why," Jackie said. "I don't know what you turn into, but I've seen the Teddy Bear, the Handbag, and the Pussy Cat and so far I'm three for three, bitch. Let Tracy go or we can make it four for four."

West stopped laughing as quickly as she stopped a human heart. Meat Fury clouded the purity of her soul. Filled her mouth with pathetic Meat Taunts.

"You want her?" West challenged. "Sure. Which half do you want?"

It was Jackie's turn to laugh. "That's good. East said something like that to me too. Told me she'd leave me piece by piece on the side of the road. But you should know, that ended with me dropping an engine block in her lap."

"And that's not all I did," Jackie pressed while West's cold blood boiled. "I made your Alligator brother shit shotgun pellets. And don't even get me started on how stupid Yogi looked after I put his eyes out."

Jackie actually closed his eyes then and swiped at the air in a crude mockery of a blind man.

When he opened his eyes again, West was already in motion.

The Shark had lost its hold on the Meat Word for "revenge." She couldn't pick her siblings out of a line up.

Killing Jackie. Shutting his filthy Meat Mouth once and for all. That was all West knew now.

It flung Tracy aside like an afterthought. The singer screamed. Jackie had a brief glimpse of Tracy's startled, terrified, eyes and then she was sailing past him, bound for the picture window separating them from the beach outside.

He could still hear Tracy screaming, right up until the sound of shattering glass cut her off.

She didn't scream anymore after that.

Dead. Jackie knew it. Deep down, he'd expected it. From the beginning, he'd only had the faintest delusions about somehow getting Tracy out of this alive. Now, he didn't even have that. All he had was West baring down on him.

Its human shroud split and withered with every step she took. Its skin turned blue. Its head bulged out in a large wedge. Its limbs lengthened and her fingers sharpened.

All the better to rip my head off with.

Jackie reached out and knocked the stereo into Tracy's reflection pool first.

The room's speaker system might have been a ten thousand dollar installation, but the stereo that it originated from was still the second hand stereo that Tracy had bought to listen to her first demo CD. It was a sentimental, scratched up piece of crap that didn't even have an iPod dock.

And it was still plugged into the wall.

The Buddhist reflecting pool was contained in a square stone basin. Pushing the stereo in the pool should have done nothing. The stone border of the pool should have kept the electrical surge completely contained.

And it would have, if Jackie hadn't pulled at the drainage plug at the base of the pool. Just a little bit, just enough for water to leak slowly but steadily out onto the floor. West might have even heard the trickle of running water… maybe, if Jackie didn't have the music turned up so loud.

But it hadn't. And the Shark was too consumed by its hatred for Jackie to realize the floor beneath its bare feet was soaking wet.

The stereo fell into the water and the shrieking of the guitar turned into a different sound. The speakers loosed a stuttering squeal of protest as the machine drowned and electricity surged out of it. The voltage spread through the pool, jumped through the loose seal, raced through the water puddled on the floor, and then leapt up into West.

The Shark never knew what hit it. One second West was sloughing off the last of her Meat Shape, Jackie's throat inches from its grasp.

The next, white light claimed it. A massive hand, larger than even its own, wrapped around West's heart and *squeezed.*

The shock hit Jackie the same way. There was no spastic flopping as the voltage hit him. Only a giant vice squeezing him tighter and tighter. It seized his heart and crushed the air from his lungs.

He didn't suffer West's blinding light, though. He saw everything. He saw the Shark in the throes of electrocution. Its blue skin turned black. Smoke began to waft off of its hide.

He knew the same thing must be happening to him as well. And if it hurt her even half as badly as it hurt him, then he'd gotten all he could have hoped for.

Before the surging current overloaded his brain, before everything became darkness Jackie had time for one final thought.

Thank you! Goodnight!

36

Tracy was not dead.

She would have been if she'd smashed headfirst into the plate glass window, but West's careless throw had actually pitched Tracy into the six-foot potted Bodhi she kept in the corner of the room. Tracy had hit the tree, and it had been the tree that smashed through the window. Tracy rolled across the beach with little more to show for it than some scratches and a mouthful of sand.

She found her feet again with none of her dancer's grace and glanced back over her shoulder to see if the freak-blonde with the teeth was coming after her, checking only to see just how quickly she needed to run.

The sight of Jack convulsing sent her running, faster than she'd ever ran in her entire life.

But she didn't run away. She ran back into the house; not through the meditation room, where Jackie vibrated on the floor and the air reeked of ozone and burning flesh. She came in through the next room over, the guest room deck with the sliding door. The glass door was locked, but she smashed a deck chair through the glass pane and staggered inside.

Please, Tracy prayed. *Please.* She stumbled back into the hallway, where the lights flickered overhead. She burst into the garage and frantically clawed things away from the walls. Life jackets. Beach chairs. She flung her bike across the garage.

It's here. It has to be. He was the one that showed it to me!

She hadn't been paying attention of course. Convinced she would never need it. Much more interested in how good he looked without-

There! She pushed aside her surfboard and there it was. The electrical panel. Tracy flung it open and flipped circuit breakers at random. The crackling continued. Jesus Christ, it went on and on, no matter how many breakers she flipped. It was only a matter of seconds but there seemed to be hundreds of switches. Thousands.

And none of them would ever, *EVER*, be the right one.

…And then, silence. The whole house was quiet and dark.

Tracy ran back to the mediation room. Still no sound, except for her panting, desperate breath.

And her screams.

"Jack!? JACK!?"

She stood in the doorway and only the steady pattering of leaking water from the pool received her. Without power, the room had taken on a shadowy blue pallor that looked to Tracy like death. The stench was no better. Everything inside reeked of burnt meat.

Tracy entered the room knowing that Jack had already left.

Two solitary mounds awaited her. The one closer to the door was massive, and not… Jesus, not human. The blonde woman, the psychopath, was nowhere to be seen. There was only this gigantic thing with a misshapen lump of a fin rising from its back. Looking at its hulking arms, Tracy remembered the sheer power that had sent her flying through the air. Here it was. Here was the true body that went with the teeth.

Gone now, though. Nothing but a fried husk in its place.

Tracy still gave it a wide berth. She wished dearly that she could turn around. Simply go back upstairs and run from the graveyard that her home had become.

The reason that she didn't was the crooked hand rising up against the backdrop of the Pacific Ocean.

Tracy knelt beside the gnarled, crooked figure. His broken arm lay flat at his side, but the "good" arm was frozen upwards at the elbow. In some places, his skin was burnt black. In others, the skin had peeled away and then the flesh underneath had burned until it was little more than dried jerky over bone.

Tracy took hold of that hand and cradled it in both of her own. There was residual heat from the electric current there, but it was a poor substitute for the warmth of his touch.

"Make sure he knows that you blame him." That's what her attacker

had wanted. She wanted Tracy's fate to be his fault.

"It was," Tracy whispered. "You did it." She kissed Jack's forehead. The skin beneath her lips felt all wrong- dry and sickly smooth.

"You saved me, Jack."

That was the only thing Jack was responsible for. Everything else was because of that blonde monster.

And you! Don't let her take all the credit, Tracy! Don't forget, Jack could have been right here on your couch instead of out getting mixed up in… well, I guess we'll never know what! Because he's dead! Thanks to you! Make sure you remember that when you have to start explaining this to people!

As if she could ever forget. The need for coke… pills, anything that would take the edge off her grief, clawed at the back of her mind. Her pain was a living creature, and it screamed for something to sooth it to sleep.

I won't, she swore. She clung to Jack's rigid hand, as if it could anchor her to the Earth, but the need still pulled at her. Grief, addiction, guilt, and raw nerves rose together and screamed out in one voice to be sated.

Tracy squeezed her eyes shut and tried to hide from the need. She found anger and seized on it.

It's really that freak's fault. That bitch. That THING.

Tracy rounded on the twisted hulk of the dead creature and struck it with both fists. The tremendous bulk didn't even shudder at the blow, but she didn't care. All she cared about was that when she hit it she didn't feel the need to snort or scream anymore. All she needed was to keep pouring her feelings out against the monster's dead flank.

Tracy hit it again and again. She battered its side until her knuckles split and her blood ran down the scorched earth of its side. Eyes blurry with tears, she struck West's carcass again and again. Her blood ran quicker and thicker as she added to the river with every punch she threw. It flowed until a single droplet coursed over a tooth and dropped into the Shark's mouth.

West opened its eyes.

The Shark rose up, flecks of charred skin flecking loose like black snow. Its roar was a grating bellow, made all the harsher for the burnt throat it escaped from. Tracy screamed and fell back on her haunches. She scrambled away with the Shark lurching after her.

The electric shock had turned the Queen Predator into a shambling, haunted house wreckage. Its dried flesh had peeled back, permanently exposing its teeth in a skull as black as a house-fire corpse. It shambled forward with a body twisted by heat and agony into something even more nightmarish than it had already been.

It came forward faster than Tracy could crawl back. Its claws closed around her leg from knee to ankle. Shriveled but still so powerful.

Tracy screamed. "Help!" she shrieked. She clawed at the damp stone floor and found no purchase. "Help me, please!" she screamed.

There was no one to hear her.

There was only that gaping mouth, drawing ever closer.

37

Backstage, Jackie Galindo slouched further down into the cheap folding chair. It was just metal, not even so much as a cushion under his ass, but it would do for the moment. He was too wasted to even make it as far as his dressing room. The performance he had just put on… it had been the most demanding show of his entire life. He barely even remembered playing a note.

We finished with Death on Contact, *I remember that much.* And only that much. Everything else was a blur from start to finish, right up until he collapsed in this cheap chair with the black Les Paul cradled to his chest.

Except that was wrong, wasn't it? He never played the black Les anymore. He kept it at home, waiting for the end of the world like one of the seven trumpets.

That's not what's wrong. Your hands-

The thought slipped away and he was too tired to chase it. He was so tired. And still they screamed for him. He heard them on the other side of the black stage curtains.

"JACK-IE!"

"JACK-IE!"

He knew what they wanted. They wanted another encore. Always one more. One more song. One more anthem. One more promise that the impossible could always be overcome.

But it's enough. I've done my part. I don't have anything else to give.

"Excuse me, Mr. Galindo?"

The stagehand lingered just beyond the dim glow of the back of house lights. All Jackie saw was a silhouette in a headset. "Mr. Galindo? Your car's waiting for you, sir."

Finally.

Jackie committed blasphemy and used his guitar as a crutch, just for a moment, just to get back on his feet, and he swore that he'd polish it as soon as he got home.

First though, he needed to get home.

Actually, all he needed to do was get to the car and then his driver would take care of the rest. All Jackie had to do was get into the backseat and drift off. When he awoke, he'd be home.

"JACK-IE!"

"JACK-IE!"

The roar of the crowd would not let him go. It held him in place, snared him with a hundred thousand thin strands woven together into a cable as thick as a ship's anchor chain.

"Mr. Galindo?" The stagehand pressed. "The car's not going to wait. It's time to go."

But they're calling me.

...And I won't let them down.

Without realizing it, he'd slung the guitar back over his shoulder. He spared one last glance for the stagehand, the one whose face was still hidden in the backstage gloom.

"Tell the car to go ahead without me," he said.

It would seem he had enough left for one more song after all.

38

West had become almost a non-entity. It had lost any pretense of its Meat Mind. It had lost the brutal magnificence of its True Self. It had forgotten about Jackie. It had forgotten about its siblings.

Pain drove West now. Pain was all it knew and pain was all it wanted to spread. This Meat Girl, wailing and cringing, would do just fine. West reeled her towards the halo of its teeth.

Something stone and angular struck it behind the knee. In West's weakened condition, the one blow was enough. The Shark pitched forward. Tracy scrambled back, narrowly avoiding the creature's bulk as it fell.

Jackie rose up behind; his primal snarl all the more inhuman by the cruel mangling of his burns. His eyes burned dark fire in his blackened skull.

He had Tracy's Buddha statue in his misshapen hands. 35 pounds of solid marble. He hefted it over his head and brought it down on West's back. The

Shark's tough hide, softened by the voltage, pulped beneath statue's weight.

Jackie lifted the statue again. Unlike West, Jackie knew no pain. He was beyond it. His broken arm felt nothing. He swung the stone bludgeon in a sideways arc and hit West again. The Shark's dorsal fin peeled off like a wet scab. West roared. Jackie gibbered and struck again.

"Take the wheel, Diana!" he raved. "My hands are a little full at the moment!" West swung its massive head around and Jackie was there with the Buddha to meet it. He crushed its eye and caved in the side of the Shark's head.

West flopped onto its back. The water beneath it tinged red with blood. Jackie lifted the statue again.

West kicked out and caught him in the thigh with a glancing blow. Diminished as she was, the blow was still an equalizer for every shot Jackie had landed. Jackie's leg snapped in half and dropped him flat on his face.

The Shark loosed a deep, wet-sounding gurgle. It retched. Blood bubbled up from its ruptured innards.

The Shark struggled to suck in air, wishing that it was cold, clear water instead.

Soon. Kill them first.

Yes. Both of them. The Shark got to its knees.

"Here, fishy, fishy, fishy."

The taunting voice came from the darkness where West's smashed eye no longer saw.

The pain followed soon after.

Jackie pitched forward, propelling the Buddha statute in front of him like a battering ram and smashing it right into the Shark's jaw. West's teeth shattered. Its fearsome maw crumbled like rock salt.

West's spirit broke with her teeth. There was no urge to murder now. If it could formulate a thought at all, all it would have asked was... *how?* How had this Meat Thing risen time and time again? How did he absorb so much punishment and constantly come back for more?

And if Jackie could have heard the question, he would have had an answer ready and waiting.

"Because I'm a Rock Star."

The Shark crawled away. Towards the sea. Towards shelter. It left a wake of blood in its path.

And in that wake, Jackie Galindo followed. West may have lost its desire for revenge, but Jackie Galindo was a burnt, bloody wraith brought back from the dead to seek nothing but revenge.

The marble Buddha lay at his feet, but he didn't need it anymore. Not when he had his eyes fixed on the gash where West's fin used to be. The red, diamond shaped gouge stood out from its blackened back like a bullseye.

Jackie dove for it. He landed on the shark's back. His good hand groped along the charred flesh of the Shark's back and then finally found the red opening where it's fin used to be. He *pushed*.

West bellowed and sprayed blood. It felt the hand invading its being, questing fingers separating flesh as it pressed deep into the Shark's chest cavity. The pain was excruciating, but the Shark was powerless to defend itself. It had nothing left.

Jackie did. He buried his good arm up to the elbow in West's viscera. He pushed through meat and blood until, finally, he brushed against something inside of the Shark that pulsed with rapid, frightened speed.

At last, he raved. *The heart of the matter!*

Jackie closed his fist around the Shark's heart. The organ was large, the size of a 30 ounce steak, and it struggled against his grip as Jack squeezed tighter around it.

But you're not fighting hard enough, bitch. I got yours before you got mine.

He pulled. West howled as something came loose inside of it. The surging typhoon in its chest, its power and its fury, was suddenly ...gone. The Meat had taken it and left West with nothing. The Shark slumped down, drifting lower and further, like a tide being pulled away by some unseen moon.

And then there was only Jackie, standing over the Shark's corpse with its heart clutched in his hand.

He waited.

He needed to be sure.

His smashed, crooked leg screamed in protest and, still, he waited.

"…Jackie?" Trish asked.

He only shook his head. Not yet.

Finally, some internal instinct told him he'd waited long enough.

The Shark was dead.

"Jackie?"

And, like the laughter of Angels, Tracy's voice. Somehow, *somehow*, he had done it. He'd saved her. Tracy was safe. He could lift the ten-ton weight of his head and he could see Tracy's blue eyes looking back at him. Even with the pain and fear that still lingered there, they were clear and they were unquestionably hers.

That was all he needed.

Jackie fell.

He didn't feel wet, even sprawled out on the soaking floor. He didn't feel Tracy's hands rolling him onto his back. He could see her lips moving, but he couldn't hear words.

Kiss me, he thought. *I'll feel that. I'll never be so gone I can't feel that.*

And then it was too late.

Jackie Galindo went into the black.

<u>39</u>

I ask Jackie what he would have become if he wasn't a musician.

"Pieces," he says with a laugh. "When I was in high school, I spent all my time doing only two things- playing rock and roll with my band and doing HVAC repairs with my dad. One day we're on a job and I knocked something called a thermocouple out of an oil heater without realizing it. I'm sitting there for like five minutes, just doing my thing, and all of a sudden my dad comes running over. And I mean RUNNING. He slams the emergency shut-off and tells me that in another five minutes that thing would've blown up and put both of our charred asses all the way out by the beach."

Jackie laughs again, like the idea of getting incinerated by an explosion was all good fun. "My old man handed me a $100 bill and then fired me on the spot. 'Keep playing your guitar,' he said. 'I'd rather you blow out your ear drums than bring you home to your mother in a jar'."

"So you're saying Rock and Roll saved your life?" I ask.

"Still hung up on that Death Trip, eh?" Jackie responds.

"I can't help it," I tell him. "I'm old enough to remember people saying Alice Cooper was converting children to Satan. And then it was Motley Crue. Marilyn Manson. *You.* Ever since Elvis, you've had people calling Rock and Roll the decay of modern society and you've had journalists like me stepping up to tell them that they're wrong. And now here you come and tell me that they're right!"

Jackie almost looks wounded. "I never said Rock and Roll was the decay of modern society," he protests. "Rock and Roll's been keeping society going since before we called it Rock and Roll."

"Keeping society alive by killing people?"

"Keeping society alive by making people not afraid to risk their lives," Jackie corrects. "Not every death trip makes it to the final destination. That's the beauty of it. Sometimes you go balls to the wall... and you live. That's the real reason people love Rock and Roll. There's no quit in it. It's pure willpower distilled down into a guitar chord. Yes, there's risks with that. There's people that die young and people that die broke. There are guys who risk everything and lose... but there are also people that win. And some of those winners, important ones, wouldn't have made it as far as they did if they didn't have Rock and Roll telling them to keep going."

"So, you're saying that Rock and Roll is actually the Life Trip... it's just that you have to take the Death Trip to make it there.

"You like road trips, Djavan?" Jackie asks. "I do. So let me tell you, I speak from experience when I say that the best trips are the ones where you have no clue where you're gonna wind up. You're just out there enjoying the ride."

I take a minute to chew this over. This idea of Rock and Roll as Tony Robbins masquerading in the Devil's cape. I can't take too long, because my hour with Jackie Galindo is almost up.

Then, I ask him my final question.

"Would you be offended if I said that I think you've been talking out of your ass for this entire interview?"

Jackie leans back and folds his deceptively strong arms across his emaciated chest. His green and black painted face cracks open in its widest grin yet.

"Not at all. I'd congratulate you on being the first journalist all day to call me on my bullshit."

40

Jackie Galindo came out of the black.

First thing in the morning these days, that was the best he could do. Once upon a time, he could kill a gallon of whiskey and then wake up seven hours later, clear-headed, fully charged, and ready to do it all over again. But now, waking up was a slow process. He rose up to consciousness reluctantly, like an unwilling animal dragged out from its burrow. There was now at least a full minute of lag time between the tightening pain behind his eyelids and the first conscious awareness that he was once again awake.

He sat up. The cane waited for him beside his bed. It was an improvement from the walker, which was an improvement over the wheelchair, which was an upgrade over the two months he spent in a hospital bed, but he still hated the sight of it.

On impulse, he swung his legs out and onto the floor. He stood, really stood on his own, for the first time in eighteen months. He had just enough time to feel accomplished before his knee buckled. Jack groped for the nightstand. His club of a left hand briefly caught the corner and then slipped off just as quickly. He hit the ground and cried out. His shoulder creaked, but mercifully held without splintering.

Ear to the floor, he could feel the vibration of feet pounding through the floor.

"Jack!" a voice screamed from down the hall. "Jack, what happened!?"

"I'm fine!" he shouted back. As if his assurance meant anything. The vibrations through the floor didn't slow, and his door flew open with no less force. Trish burst into the room as if she expected to see that his head had spontaneously combusted.

"I'm alright," he said, even though he had to look up from the floor to say it.

"Right. I'll just go back to my Sudoku and leave you to it, then." She got him under the armpits and deadlifted him up, taking the brunt of his weight until he could get hold of his cane.

"Lose some weight or use the cane, Jack. One or the other." Trish may have sounded cold, but her gaze warmed once she was sure he wouldn't be taking another fall anytime soon. "You want an early lunch or a late breakfast?" she asked.

"What were you planning before I got up?"

"Shut up and tell me what you want," his sister groused.

Jackie sighed. "Can I get breakfast?" he said.

"Of course you can," she responded with exaggerated dignity. "Eggs?"

"Thanks, Trish."

Jack watched her leave. It occurred to him, as it did every morning, that he needed to find some present for her that she wouldn't be able to refuse. He'd considered putting a Tesla in her driveway, sending the whole family to Australia for two weeks, and putting both of her kids through a lifetime of private school.

No matter what he came up with, nothing seemed good enough.

He stumped his way down to the kitchen. His phone waited there on the kitchen counter and he made his daily check-in with what he thought of as the World Outside. The usual offers were there. They piled up in his phone every day just as sure as the tide came in. Offers to front new bands. Offers to put his name on a ghost-written tell-all book. The occasional inventor looking for someone to endorse a guitar you could play without working fingers.

Sometimes for fun he liked to compare the contract terms to his hospital bills. The licensing fees for this hologram tour would equal the two months he spent in the ICU and the eighteen months of physical therapy. And here was an offer for a two-album deal. Even before royalties it was enough to cover the stem cell treatments they'd used to rebuild his circulatory system.

The only messages he ignored outright were the ones campaigning to be his new agent.

"Jack!" Trish shouted.

He snapped up from his phone; Trish stared at him with wide, alarmed eyes. Jack touched his nose, too see if it was bleeding again, but his fingers came back dry.

"Jack, your hand!"

He looked down and finally understood. He'd put a hand on the counter to steady himself while he checked his phone. Looking down now, he realized that he'd stuck his hand smack-dab in the middle of a half-eaten cherry danish and hadn't felt a thing.

He didn't feel the rough touch of the paper towel as he cleaned his hand off either. His left hand was little more than a crude replica carved by a poor craftsman. It didn't move, the details didn't look right, and Jackie didn't feel a thing, no matter what happened to it.

"Be more careful," Trish chastised.

"Be more sanitary," he shot back.

She threw an avocado pit at him. "Not that I need to justify anything to you, but that was from Lucy's breakfast. It's her responsibility to clean it up."

"Where is the kid?" Jack asked, and was then answered by an uneven, but not inept, stumble of guitar chords from out on the deck. Jackie listened approvingly.

"She's got that G down," he said. He picked up the danish with his good hand and took a bite. "And she doesn't give a damn about her bad reputation. You might have a mini-Joan Jett on your hands."

Trish set an omelet down at the table. "Are you going to critique my parenting all day, or are you going to go see your… friend?"

The grin slipped from Jack's face. *If* he was going, then he had to start getting ready soon. It took him longer to shower and dress now than it used to. And as for driving, it would also seem like he had less lead in his foot than he used to.

"I'm going," Jack said. Eating was still a battle. His "good" hand could only tenuously grasp a fork between his ring and middle finger, but he nevertheless dug in as quickly as he could manage.

Trish didn't say anything. She wanted to- Jack could see the words building up in her cheeks, but she kept it to herself.

Jack put his plate in the sink and stood at the crossroads. If he was really going to leave, he'd stump his way back down the hall to the bathroom.

Instead, he went out onto the porch.

I can still make it if I skip the shower.

A lie. And one he might have chastised himself for if the sight on the porch hadn't stolen every thought from his head.

"Hey, Uncle Jack," Lucy said. She barely looked at him, but not for the reason that most people avoided looking at him. Lucy wasn't bothered by the scars. She'd been the first one to kiss him after he woke up in the hospital. Sometimes, when her mom wasn't around, she called him Uncle Deadpool.

No, the reason Lucy wouldn't look at him was because she was too focused on her fingers. Just listening to her strum, he could tell that she was trying to switch from a D7 to a C major, but she couldn't quite make the move. It was the auditory equivalent of someone trying to hop between two stones and falling just short.

Jackie watched her try, hair tucked back in a ponytail so it wouldn't get in her eyes, tongue sticking out at the corner of her mouth as she stumbled over the transition again and again. Only when it was clear that she had no intention of quitting until she got it did he say, "You're leading with the wrong finger. Move your third finger first, and then the second'll follow."

Lucy didn't say thanks. She never did when he gave her guitar advice, but she always listened without question. She didn't get it on the first try, or even the second, but even the slip-ups sounded better. By the fourth try, she had the move down nicely and then she even tacked a few more notes behind it for a little extra "fuck you."

"Where'd you get that guitar?" Jack asked.

"One of your boxes in the basement. I was looking for picks." He was little more than a ghost to her again. Reality to her was only in notes and chords waiting to be untangled. "Is that okay?" she asked, likely in deference to some small voice that still worried about getting in trouble, but Jack could tell that she really didn't give a damn if she was.

Jackie smiled. "It's fine. Talk to you later, Loopy."

She only grunted.

Jack hobbled back inside, content to leave the six-year-old alone with the seven thousand dollar 1968 Les Paul.

It was in good hands.

He decided to chance the shower. But quickly. He had to be quick. Both for time and because for where his mind might wander in the solitude of-

Tracy has the 5 month sobriety token clenched in her hand. She turns it over constantly while she speaks.

It occurred to him, not for the first time, that the guitar wasn't the only thing that might be better off without him.

But the guitar wasn't asking to see him again.

Tracy was.

"I wanted to thank you," she tells him.

Jack shakes his head. Even six months later, the slight movement is enough to make his taut skin bite. "That thing only knew your name because of me," he says.

"The only reason I'm alive is because you came back for me."

She looks him in the eye then. Her blue eyes are clear, the way he always remembered them. At that moment, he could touch her with the dead lump of his left hand and all feeling would come rushing back the moment he caressed her skin.

He doesn't try. They talk a little more, but there's nothing else to say. Or maybe there is, but there's no point in saying it. He won't see her again.

Until yesterday when he checked his phone and saw a day old text message waiting for him.

`Hey. Can we get coffee sometime?`

He sent a response hours later, obsessing over every word and starting over more times than he could count.

`Still want to? Tomorrow good?`

Other than a few minor details, that was all they said to each other. She hadn't said why she wanted to see him and he hadn't asked.

He stepped out of the shower and got a good look at himself in the mirror. No need for monster makeup now. There wasn't enough money or experimental treatments in the world to completely repair what he'd done to himself. He didn't have eyebrows. He didn't have lips. Discolored burn scars canvased his entire body. One ear was permanently forked.

There was a pause in his train of thought while he looked in the mirror, a gap saved for bitter assuredness that the only time he could share a table with the most beautiful woman on the planet would be at a fundraiser for a burn ward. *Attention ladies and gentlemen, we're being momentarily held at the station while we wait for bad jokes about the Phantom of the Recording Studio.*

…Except, the bitter thoughts never came.

He had no idea why Tracy wanted to see him, and he finally realized that it didn't matter. The world was the same as it always was- a poker hand with all the cards face down. Whether or not he won didn't matter nearly as much as knowing that he was still at the table to see how it played out.

Maybe Tracy just wanted to talk.

Maybe she wanted everything.

No matter what happened, Jackie still had Rock and Roll.

He could take whatever the world threw at him.

ABOUT THE AUTHOR

Sean McDonough is the author of two previous books, available at most online retailers. He lives in New York with his wife and wonderful daughter. Follow him on Facebook at https://www.facebook.com/houseoftheb oogeyman.